PRAISE FOR TWELVE

Amy H says:
I loved this story. It was a unique take on the Twelve Dancing Princesses story, but this isn't your mother's fairy tale. This story took a darker...look at the story. I read it in one sitting and couldn't bring myself to put it down.

DMCI says:
Twelve is certainly is a fractured retelling of the Dancing Princesses tale. It's a unique perspective, told well and combines the elements of classic fairy tales and contemporary romance. I was drawn into the story and couldn't put it down. I look forward to reading more.

The Naughty Librarian says:
Twelve is a really sad story with a cute ending. The story begins with a young boy… Years go by. The twist is part of what made this little story endearing.

Casey L says:
Twelve is a quirky twisted tale of the Twelve Dancing Princesses. Raised in an unconventional manner, these strong princesses take their destined fates into their own hands and live their lives how they want. Family can be a strange concept to many - loyalty and honesty vie against duty and power.
This story is a daring look at what a family can be.

Twelve

A Flip-Flopped Fairy Tale

USA Today Bestselling Author
Savannah Verte

TWELVE
A Flip-Flopped Fairy Tale

By Savannah Verte

Published by
Eclectic Bard Books
USA

This novel is a work of fiction. Any resemblance to actual persons, living or deceased is coincidental. The characters, names, plots, or incidents within are the product of the author's imagination. References to actual events or locations are included to give the fiction a sense of reality.

Copyright 2018, Savannah Verte.

All rights reserved. No part of this may be reproduced, stored, or transmitted in any form, by any means without written consent from Savannah Verte.

Cover design: Funky Book Design, 2017.

Dedication

For My King...

For understanding that who I am is who I am. For giving me free reign to let my crazy out.

And,

For supporting my journey, wherever the road goes.

LONELY BOY

Lyford Rousseau was anointed King at the ripe old age of ten. The only child of his parents, their premature demise left him with no choices, few allies, and one sprawling kingdom to run, with no understanding of what that actually entailed. He was only a boy after all.

His father's vizier, Armen, was his only influence as he assumed his future. Then again, he'd been one of the few people present in his life before that fateful day as well. It would be ages before Lyford learned that the accident that took his parents was planned, and at the direction of Armen, but that's another story. Lyford ascended to the throne oblivious to the deceit.

Lyford got a crash course in what it meant to be king. Soon enough, he found that he resented the responsibility, longing for the days when he could be a child. They were long gone. What he missed most, was sneaking away to the kitchens to play with Bryn. Their days of cobble-skip were the only happy memories he could recount.

His parents had never really been affectionate. Fully consumed with their status, and the trappings of wealth, they'd had little time for Lyford. He was heir to the throne, and a token of the kingdom, but not a beloved child. Armen, though the sole permanent adult fixture in Lyford's young life, was a poor substitute. His role was as an educator, counselor, and guide, not parent, friend, or confidant.

The early years of his reign became an unpleasant blur. Until he was of age, Armen had responsibility for all of the decisions. Lyford was merely a figurehead. Upon his eighteenth birthday, he would be expected to fully embrace his role, and the responsibilities it entailed. If he could be ready by then was anyone's guess, though if any would ask him, he was certain the answer was no.

Reviewing the scrolls, it seemed to Lyford that the coffers were thin, though who, or what, was to blame for that, he could not ascertain. It could easily have been the result of his parent's lavish lifestyle. He remembered well the evenings when he was left in his quarters with instructions not to emerge. Watching from the window, he saw the line of carriages as they arrived, people emerging in smart and sparkling finery. He couldn't help but hear the parties he was never allowed to attend.

Twelve

Armen's counsel now was that he would need to endeavor to refill the funds if he were to entice a bride someday. Alone in his room later, Lyford's stomach turned as he thought back over the conversation.

"Why would I want to entice a bride?" He'd moaned.

"You are young yet, but one day you will not be, and the future of your kingdom depends on there being an heir to ascend to the throne after your time. Do you believe they grow on trees?" Armen chided, clucking his tongue at the young king.

"But do I have to have a bride for that? Isn't there another way?" Lyford complained. "If my parents are any example, I don't want what they had."

Armen laughed robustly. "One day you will change your mind. One day, it will be exactly everything that you think of. Not perhaps…" He paused with a wry grin, "for the public display, but more so perhaps for the private moments."

"Private moments?! Private, as in, alone?" Lyford groused, uncertain what exactly the implications were.

Armen did his best to hide his amusement. His best wasn't very good. "Yes, alone. You will understand better when you are older. For now, take my word for it, it is something that you will want."

Savannah Verte

Years later, Lyford recalled the conversation clearly as he struggled with himself. Since his ascension, he'd had next to no interaction with most of the staff in the castle. When he was younger, he didn't care, or recognize, that there was a difference between them. The line between royal and non—royal was made exceedingly clear soon after his anointment and crowning. He'd been all but forbidden from seeing Bryn, actually the only one he missed. He hadn't realized how much so until he saw her again.

Passing a doorway, he caught a glimpse of her as she spoke to someone else. He would have known it was her, even if the other party hadn't addressed her by name. She was changed, but in many ways, she was the same. Her long, flowing golden locks nearly reached her hips, even in the braid that bound them. Her dimples too, were exactly as he remembered them, though he didn't remember noticing them so much before. Even her voice was familiar to how he had recalled it in his mind.

Twelve

The rest...the rest was a very different person than the girl he remembered. She had grown up. She was still shorter than he was, but her form was no longer similar to his, like it had been so long ago. She had curves. He stared far longer than he probably should have, but still managed to make his escape before he was noticed. Several steps down the hall, he was uncomfortable to realize a physical response to seeing her.

Pausing his retreat, he took account of himself. His palms were damp, as was his brow. His heart-beat was accelerated, and his breath was short. Most disconcerting was a stirring, an uncomfortable stirring at the apex of his thighs. His thoughts were a whirl as he set out to find Armen.

"What is this madness?" He demanded as he burst into the vizier's quarters.

Armen turned slowly, looked the young king up and down, noticing the flush. "Madness? I'm afraid you'll have to be more specific. Have you been running?"

"No. I have not been running. Don't be funny. You are not the Jester." Lyford retorted, trying to keep his panic from coming through his words. "I was standing still but my heart is racing, my breath is short, and my palms are wet as though I did not dry them after washing. What. Is. This. Madness?!" He enunciated his perplexing predicament.

Armen tilted his head. "*Where* were you standing when this happened?"

"In the hallway."

His brows furrowed as he considered the information. "By yourself?" He asked, certain that he was missing a piece of the puzzle.

"Yes! I was by myself." Lyford grumbled.

"Then I don't know what this could possibly be. If you weren't alone, I could possibly glean more from knowing whom else was present, or what was happening. But, alone, solo? No, there is no explanation." Armen countered, returning to his tables on the desk before him nonchalantly.

Lyford debated before releasing an exasperated sigh, stomping his foot to draw the vizier's attention back to him. "Fine. I was alone, but I could see other people. Does that change your answer?"

Armen smirked to the desk before schooling his face and turning back to the young king. "It might. Who did you see?"

"Members of the staff."

Armen nodded. "I see. Anyone specific?"

"Kitchen staff."

Armen's snort was muffled, but audible. "So, you saw women."

Lyford was already tired of the interaction, wishing desperately that he had not asked, and was now ready to be finished. "Yes. I saw women. I saw Bryn." He finally admitted.

Twelve

Armen nodded knowingly. "Then I would say that this madness you speak of is your primal self, trying to tell you that you are approaching when the 'private moments' we spoke of once upon a time, might be more important."

"I've already told you that I am not interested in those." Lyford asserted defiantly.

"I know you did. I also know that one day your body and your mind may not agree."

"We'll see about that." Lyford spat before spinning on his heel and leaving the vizier's quarters. He was furious that Armen was so arrogant about potentially being right. He was more determined than ever to prove him wrong.

THIRTY YEARS

Over the next years, Lyford became more and more reclusive. He had seen Bryn multiple times, always from the distance. Each time, his reaction was the same. If anything, only the veracity of it was different, growing more profound each time.

Any hope that he would one day prove Armen wrong was dashed, and dashed again. All he needed to do, to know that he was not going to contradict Armen, was see Bryn. He soon learned that distance did nothing to erase her influence either. He was waking from sound slumber, his body contorting in response to dream images of her, night after night. Detestable as the ideal was, he needed to find a way to deal with the situation. Hating to have to ask, Armen was the only one he could query.

"Tell me about the private moments." He opened abruptly.

Twelve

"Tell you…" Armen managed before his laughter broke loose. "I see. What do you want to know?"

"Do they hurt?"

Armen fought valiantly to keep his features neutral. Mostly he managed. "Hurt? No, they hardly hurt. Why would you think such a thing?"

"Because my heart is thundering and feels like it's trying to break loose of my chest. I can't breathe. And…" Lyford hedged.

"Go on…" Armen encouraged, fairly certain he knew what was coming, but unwilling to miss Lyford's description.

"And… I know I'm not coming undone, but part of me really hurts."

Armen swallowed hard. He was aghast that this had not come up more, before, or sooner. "Have you never taken one of the staff girls for a toss?"

"What's a toss?" Lyford asked, completely befuddled.

"A toss. A roll in the hay. Bumping uglies. Getting your rocks off. Nothing? Do these phrases have no meaning to you?" Armen listed, growing more and more surprised as he watched the confusion play across the young king's face.

"Why would they?!" Lyford demanded. "All I have done since my parents died was learn how to run this kingdom. A toss? Bump uglies? Where was that in the lesson plan?" He challenged.

Somehow it had never occurred to Armen that he would be the one to have the sex talk with Lyford. Why it had escaped him, was anyone's guess. He himself had not had the conversation so to speak, but gone out into the world to learn what he wanted to know. Lyford's rigorous and regimented upbringing for the first ten years, and subsequent crash course in ruler-ship over the recent ones, had left him lacking. Armen was still struggling with the reality as his next question tumbled out indelicately. "Have you never touched yourself then?"

Lyford thought he might be sick. "Touch… Myself…" He stated as much as asked. "To bathe, yes. To relieve myself, yes. What are you asking?"

Armen was nearly certain that the latter was to void, not relief the way he was thinking. "No, I mean when it is changed, hardened, and elongated. Have you ever touched yourself?"

"Great Goddess no." Lyford nearly shouted. It was one of the few things he remembered his mother for, her explicit instructions never to touch *that* for anything else.

"You should." Armen replied matter-of-factly, obviously shocking Lyford. "Try that first. Then, we'll talk about what comes next."

Twelve

Permission given, Lyford was a quick study. Before long, he knew exactly how to relieve his angst, and need, after an encounter with Bryn. Armen was amused often by Lyford's abrupt excuses to leave a room. The young king was more than ready. And, it was time.

When he returned from his latest personal escape, Armen launched without preamble. "We need to discuss the future of your kingdom."

"How so?" Lyford asked, convincingly more relaxed than he'd been when he left, as he returned to his seat.

"The registers have regained much of their former numbers. You are in a good position now to consider taking a queen. Your subjects have been patient, but will begin to rumble if there is not a plan for the future. You have no heir. You have no queen. If anything would happen, as did with your parents, who would govern? You need to consider your subjects."

"But I don't want a queen. Is there a way to go forward without one?" Lyford complained, his agitation returning.

"No. Not really. A legal heir to the throne is necessary at some point." Armen leveled.

Lyford huffed in exasperation, pushed back his chair, rose, and began pacing. "I suppose you have a plan." He challenged on a turn back from the far side of the room.

"I do."

"I'm not going to like it, am I?"

Armen shrugged. "I don't know that you will dislike it. What I have in mind would expand your kingdom twofold."

"I'm listening."

"The Coeur d'Alene kingdom across the northern border might be an option. We could perhaps propose a merger as a way to plan for the future of both. The king there is older, and has only daughters. He has no male heir to succeed him. A wedding between the families could solve that for him, and provide you a wife of your stature." Armen detailed carefully. In fact, he had been laying the seeds for this plan for many years.

"Do I have another choice?" Lyford lamented, crossing his arms over his chest.

"You always have a choice. The more important question is do you have a better choice? In my opinion, you don't."

"But what if I don't like her? What if she doesn't appeal to me?"

Twelve

Armen chuckled. "I see your priorities have shifted. What you need to understand is that this is not about what you like or don't like. It is about strategic decisions, and how best to secure the future of your kingdom, as well as satisfy the curiosities of your subjects."

"But you're saying I would be required to bed her."

"Yes. For as much, or as often, as would be required to conceive."

"Somehow it sounds like my parents' relationship." Lyford replied before realizing his thought had escaped.

"In many ways, it is just that." Armen defended, trying to remain neutral. "Your parents' marriage was also one of convenience. They did not have other children after you because you were a son. I would tell you otherwise if it would make it more palatable, but truth is truth."

"The truth is unpleasant."

"As you say. What would you like to do?"

Lyford paced back to the far wall, bracing his hands against the windowsill. Looking out across the lands, he knew he had no alternative. What he wanted, was almost certainly not an option, so he did not give it voice. Raising to his full height, he did not turn before speaking, trusting the words would carry across the space. "Ask the question. Maybe they will say no." He silently hoped.

Savannah Verte

The dispatched courier returned so quickly that Lyford thought his head might spin. Then again, he did not know that Armen had been priming the situation behind his back. The resounding acceptance of the offer left Lyford in a funk. The Coeur d'Alene king, Leopold, accepted, pledging his daughter Grace with one amendment. If no male heir was born to ascend over both kingdoms within thirty years' time, the bargain was void.

"Then what?" Lyford demanded. "What if there is no son? What if there are no children at all?"

Armen bit hard on his tongue to stay his grin before looking up to respond, scanning the scroll as a diversion. "According to this, in that event, your kingdom would become his."

Reinforcements

The marriage between Lyford and Grace was celebrated, but only attended by a small handful of witnesses. Once the nuptials were complete, the documents merging the two kingdoms under the agreed-upon terms were signed by the couple, as well as by her father Leopold on behalf of his kingdom. The wax seals were still setting as the couple retired to their quarters.

Keeping with an ancient tradition, a crowd gathered in the courtyard below the window, waiting for the bloodied bedsheets. The couple fumbled their way through the consummation of their union, handing off the linens for display before parting company. They had been some of the most awkward moments of Lyford's life.

Grace was older than he was by several years. She was not unpleasant to look upon, though in his mind he could not reconcile her as anything other than a substitute for Bryn. He would never admit that it had taken him calling Bryn to mind to be able to complete the task. He knew it was inconsiderate, but he reconciled it with himself that this was a duty now, not a match for love or attraction.

Before long on the calendar, though a seeming eternity to Lyford, Grace was pregnant. In his mind, it was a reprieve. He would not be forced to attend her that way again until after the child was born, if ever. He returned to the business of ruling his kingdom, leaving her to fend for herself.

When her pregnancy began to have challenges, she was put to bed. Other than rising to bathe, or to move to a chair to sit, she was restricted to bed until after the birth. Lyford was consulted, but only to inform, he was not part of the decision.

"What do they want me to do about it?" He asked Armen, exasperated by the development.

Armen shrugged, mildly irritated himself. "It seems that they don't."

"I cannot attend her every moment of the day. It was all I could do to attend her to get pregnant in the first place." Lyford groused, slamming his fist upon the table.

"Perhaps one of the staff can attend her." Armen offered.

"Or perhaps one of her staff, or family members, can come attend her. The coffers have swelled because I have kept the costs down. Taking on more staff is not part of that solution." Lyford

Twelve

countered. "The agreement did not include expanding the household beyond a child."

Armen raised an eyebrow. "You seem to feel quite strongly about it."

Lyford glared. "Let's just say I have a new appreciation and understanding of why my youth was the way it was."

"And you would repeat that?" Armen challenged, genuinely curious.

"Yes. And, no. I do not intend for my child to be as unseen as I was, but I also do not intend to deplete the wealth of my kingdom before he arrives."

Armen nodded. "As you wish. Perhaps, I can reach out to her father."

"Do that." Lyford stated adamantly. "Perhaps this will all be an unnecessary discussion sooner than later."

Armen did not bait him to try to understand what his thought process might be. He was amused to see so much of Lyford's father in him. His thought process was almost a mirror of the days when he himself was conceived and his mother the one ordered to rest. How intriguing that the fates would repeat the pages.

Elba arrived with the return courier. She was a trusted nursemaid for the Coeur d'Alene family. She would see Grace through the pregnancy, and stay on after to aid with caring for the child. In many ways it was a better solution than what they had hoped for when the request was sent. After introductions were made to the primary staff responsible for the queen and her daily needs, Elba was escorted to Grace's quarters to begin her duties.

Lyford and Armen breathed a sigh of relief in unison. The queen would be attended, the staff would not be unduly stressed, and they could do what needed doing to oversee the newly combined kingdoms. Everything seemed to be running smoothly, and in an easy routine with the exception of a visit from Grace's father to see that everything was proceeding appropriately.

"Is she eating enough?" He challenged.

"Ask her yourself." Lyford defended. "She is neither deprived, nor forced. If she is hungry, she eats. If she is weary, she rests. If she needs anything else, your appointed nursemaid sees to it that she has her every request."

"You do not attend her?" Leopold baited, eyeing Lyford through squinted eyes.

Lyford eased back in his chair to answer the challenge. "Did you attend your queen during her pregnancies?"

"Touché." Leopold answered skeptically. "I'll see my daughter now."

As if on cue, Elba appeared to escort him to Grace's side. He remained for three days before departing for home. "When the birth becomes imminent, we will be here." He issued from his perch.

"You will be the first to know." Lyford replied, muttering under his breath after her father was away. "As if we could prevent it."

Daughters

The squall echoed through the castle in the dark hours of night. Lyford had drifted to sleep at some point as Grace's labor went on into the second day. He was nearby, but not in the room as his child was delivered. The shrill cry woke him abruptly. He jumped to his feet, paced outside the door, and waited for word.

Grace's father emerged first, clapping him on the shoulder. "Better luck next time, son. You have a beautiful daughter, but no heir to the throne."

Lyford entered after the door was opened to him. "So, it's a girl?" He asked flatly.

Elba looked up from the far side of the queen, who was obviously exhausted. She was not so much participating in helping to get herself cleaned up, as she barely managed to hold

Twelve

the baby as it suckled. "Yes, it's a girl." The nursemaid beamed. "She's quite beautiful. Would you like to see her?"

Lyford shook his head. "No. I'll see her after she's not so messy."

"As you wish." Elba replied, returning to her duties.

Lyford left the room without another comment.

"Oooo, he's a broody one." Elba muttered as she finished setting the queen to right. "Not even a glance. Not even a curiosity." She paused her lament, realizing a more important thing was lacking. "Not even a name."

Grace smiled weakly, the extended labor had worn her through. "It's okay. If he didn't name her, then I will. We will call her Aislyn."

"A more beautiful, fitting name I have never heard." Elba chimed. "If you are not able, it will be my great pleasure to introduce her, by name, to her father later."

"In time, Elba. In time."

Grace was content to dote on Aislyn. It did not bother her in the slightest that Lyford was not participating. She had no disillusion about the marriage she was in. When the request had come, she was not surprised to be the daughter chosen to fulfill the Coeur d'Alene side of the bargain.

She was the eldest, and as her father had all daughters, the closest thing to a son he had. She understood the registers and scrolls better than the scribes probably did. The amendment that was added to the acceptance, was done so with her in mind. If, there would be no male heirs to the combined kingdom, and it would in fact revert to the Coeur d'Alene family, it would do so with her at the helm. That detail was a closely guarded family secret.

She would bear Lyford's children in good faith to the agreement. But, her children would be the benefactors of their union regardless of the outcome. She knew it was tip-toeing the line of deceit, but it was the only way her family would agree. They just needed to keep the secret.

She was surprised when Lyford came to her sooner than later. "We need to try again." He opened without preamble or affection.

"I beg your pardon?" She replied, needing to clarify she had heard him clearly.

Twelve

"Again? Try again? Another baby? Perhaps you could have a boy this time." He muttered, asserting that somehow it was up to her.

Agitated, she did her best to curb her temper. "What? Right now? Did you want to hold Aislyn while we do that, or can I hand her off to Elba first?"

His face flushed. "Tonight. Just be ready." He challenged before turning for the door.

Not quite willing to give him the last word, she replied to his back. "Would that be your room? Or, mine?"

As he spun to face her, she caught the flash of rage that crossed his features before he spoke. "I don't give a damn if it's the floor. Just be ready."

Once he was gone she hissed her reply to the door. "The floor it is."

Grace's second pregnancy was significantly easier than the first. The delivery too, bore little resemblance to the first. The couple's

second child emerged with little difficulty, the sun shining brightly through the windows.

As with the first, Lyford waited in the hall. When the ruckus subsided, and the doors were opened, he entered. This time, Grace was sitting up, cooing at the small bundle in her arms. It did not escape his notice that the swaddling was pink. "It's a girl, isn't it?"

Grace glanced up, letting her smile answer his question for a moment before she responded. "Yes. It's a girl. Would you care to meet her, hold her, and perhaps name her?" She challenged sweetly, repeating Elba's invitation from the first birth.

Lyford's eye roll and quick retreat were his only response.

"What will she be called?" Elba asked gaily.

"So many choices." Grace lamented joyfully. "I believe we will honor her with my mother's namesake. She will be called Feraut."

"Beautiful. Simply, beautiful." Elba exclaimed. "Would you like to be alone now?"

"No. But, I believe I would like you to bring in Aislyn to meet her sister."

"I can certainly manage that."

Twelve

Lyford's rage was inconsolable. "Two pregnancies and two daughters…" He muttered repeatedly under his breath as he stomped through the castle. "What am I supposed to do with daughters? I need a son. Just one, one to carry on the name and secure the future. Is that really so much to ask?"

He was so busy feeding his ire that he was not paying attention to his path. Without warning, he rounded a corner and plowed Bryn to the ground. Any other chance encounter with her would have had a different result. This time, it only served to infuriate him further. He paused, only for a second, but long enough to realize it was her which was the only thing that prevented him from lashing out. Instead, he spun on his heel and took off another direction, leaving her lying across the hallway floor. He muttered a halfhearted, "Sorry." over his shoulder as he retreated.

By the time he reached the armory, his wrath had a life of its own. Without thought, or premeditation, multiple suits of armor were in pieces on the floor. The commotion brought members of the staff running. As they entered, his awareness returned. Too agitated to apologize, he glanced around the room and to the servants who had arrived. "Just clean it up." He shouted in disgust as he again retreated.

Finding Armen, he unleashed his fury. "How hard can it be to have a son?" He challenged.

The vizier laughed openly. "I'll take that to mean you have another daughter."

Lyford glared in response. Armen, though quite pleased by the news, pasted a more somber expression across his features. "I have no children. I cannot answer your question."

"That's quite unhelpful."

Armen shrugged. "I have no sage wisdom to offer as I have no experience in such matters."

"Well, something needs to change. The next child needs to be a son." Lyford all but shouted.

Armen pursed his lips to keep from smirking. "Do let me know what you change to ensure a different outcome." He countered, returning his focus to the pages he had been reading.

Lyford again stomped off. Leaving the castle, he headed for the stables. Perhaps some fresh air would clear his mind. He arrived just in time to witness a stag and mare copulating. Groaning aloud, he retreated. The last thing he needed was to see

Twelve

the animals making babies. At least, he absently thought, they appeared to be enjoying the effort.

TWINS

Months later, Grace had settled into a quiet routine. She was easily content to raise the girls well away from their father. With not a thought in her mind about trying again, she was caught off guard when Lyford came to her rooms. "I'm surprised to see you." She said when he entered.

"You shouldn't be. We do not have a son yet." He responded flatly.

"I am aware." She answered, returning her attention to other things.

"I would hope so." He said, an odd tone in his voice.

She was still trying to decipher the meaning of it when he surprised her again. Coming up behind her, she was unprepared for his advance. She was also unable to retreat or defend his actions.

Twelve

"Perhaps…" He began as he raised her skirts, "we've been doing it wrong. My horses do it this way, and I have a stable full of stags. I wonder why that is?" He continued as he adjusted her position to line up their bodies.

She knew better than to try to respond or resist, it would only make him more insistent, or possibly angry, and as it was, he never lingered to cuddle. She'd be rid of him soon enough.

The delivery was a bloodied disaster. The twin girls arrived early, and as such, were small. That was where their similarities stopped. One was fair with hair so light it was barely discernible. The other, had a full head of dark locks and a deeper skin tone. If their appearances held, anyone who didn't know they were twins would not mistake them as such.

Like every birth to date, Lyford paced the hallway waiting. Even when Elba called out for assistance, he remained beyond the door. In defiance, she made him wait unnecessarily longer because of it. She had already realized by his previous performances that it would not matter if Grace was clean or bloodied, the news of daughters would send him retreating quickly. As such, she decided to clean the queen first and let him come in after.

Before long, there was an unexpectedly gentle tapping at the door. Not wanting to be fooled, Elba called out in response instead of opening the door. "We're not quite ready yet. Another moment please."

A soft female voice called back. "I just wanted to see if you needed anything. It has been a long, quiet wait."

"We're fine." Grace called back. "Thank you for checking."

"Then what the hell is taking so long?" Lyford chimed in.

"One more minute…" Elba chimed sweetly.

"You know you will have to let him in eventually. You might as well not make him wait any longer. It does neither of us any good." Grace admonished.

Tossing the bloodied linens across the bed where he would be unable to miss them, Elba moved to the door and let him in. "Suit yourself." She directed toward him as she swept her arm across the threshold into the room. "I was trying to clean everything up first."

Lyford crossed the room to Grace. He turned his nose up at the site of the dirty sheets. Glancing to the two tiny children lying across Grace's chest to suckle, he could not tell if they were boys or girls. He hated having to ask. But, he needed to know. "Are they…?"

"Daughters." Elba announced from behind him, relishing delivering the news.

Lyford spun to face her. "Both of them? Are you sure?"

Elba's head pulled back on her shoulders at his impudence. "I've delivered enough babies in my life to know the difference. Yes, I'm certain."

Lyford began his retreat, muttering under his breath as he went. "How difficult can this be? How can they be girls once again?"

Elba waited until he was out of earshot before muttering her own answer. "Because, once again, you forgot to put the stem on the apple. How difficult can that be?" She asked the empty space where he had been.

"I heard that." Grace whispered.

Elba turned with a broad grin. "It wasn't you who I meant not to hear it."

"Oh, I know. It was funny. But, be careful. He's not a very happy person. And, I need you."

"Just so we're clear, *they* need you." Elba gestured to the two freshly swaddled bundles. "I'm only here to help."

"We're clear. Now, come meet your nieces." Grace smiled warmly. "This is Evelyn. And, this dark haired beauty, I'm going to call Raven."

Lyford seemed to disappear. Like the previous births, he had stormed off, though this time, where he went was a mystery. Even Armen couldn't find him, and he seemed to have an innate sense of the king. In truth, Lyford did not want to be found. Secreted away in a forgotten annex, he'd found the perfect spot to watch Bryn without being noticed.

From his perch behind a dusty tapestry, he watched her and wished for simpler times. What he wouldn't give for a game of cobble-skip and some laughter. He shocked himself to realize that having his parents back would rank high on his list of priorities as well, if only because none of this would be his burden to bear. He still had plenty of time to fulfill the amendment for the merger of the kingdom, but he was tired of thinking about fulfilling the merger amendment.

Somewhere in the back of his mind he clicked to a mental image where Bryn was the one bringing his children to life.

Twelve

Somehow, he didn't think he'd mind one hundred girls with her. He hated the realization that he had, in many ways, become his parents. Even thinking it, he could not find a way to change it. He was now the father to four daughters, and in truth, other than their names, he could no more tell you which was whom.

With the twins growing steadily, Grace finally felt settled enough to leave them long enough to get some fresh air alone. Armen spied her walking in the gardens. He had wondered when he would finally have an opportunity to put his latest plan into play. Pulling aside a member of the guard whom he trusted, he didn't need to say much. "Perhaps the queen would enjoy a ride."

"Lancer, or the other?"

"Your choice. Both of them are easily spooked." Armen replied quietly. "There's a storm brewing on the other side of the hills."

"I understand."

"I'll be with the king."

Without another word, they parted company.

"You shouldn't be out here alone." The guard called ahead of his approach.

Grace spun in surprise. "I didn't see you there. I was just getting some fresh air. I won't be long, promise."

"How long has it been? I can't say that I've seen you out of the castle in ages."

Grace chuckled. "It has been ages. I'm afraid I've had my hands full."

"And now?"

"Now, the babies are growing and I know they are in capable hands. Before the weather turns cold and steals the colors, I wanted to enjoy the gardens up close."

"I was going to go for a quick ride to take a couple of the horses for a stretch. They too have been cooped up. Perhaps, if we are quick, you would enjoy helping me." He offered.

Twelve

Grace was tempted. She hadn't been on horseback since before Aislyn was born. Perhaps a quick ride would be pleasant. Glancing up to the window, and her rooms beyond, she debated.

"There's weather moving in, so it would have to be quick. If you were to help me, we could do two at the same time. Maybe, we could finish even faster and you could still take a walk through the gardens." He doubled the opportunity presented.

"I have to admit a quick ride would be thrilling. It's been so long."

"Then a quick ride it will be. I already have them saddled."

Feeling mischievous, Grace gave in. "Okay then, let's go."

They were off without delay. Grace laughed at the carefree ride, relishing the feel of the wind through her hair. True to his prediction, the weather was coming in fast. Before she noticed the skies turning, they were dark and a loud clap of thunder rang out. As it did so, the horse reared up and she was thrown. She landed hard and was disoriented. It was the last sensation she recognized.

Replacement

Lyford stood abruptly when the guard rushed in. "The queen is dead."

"Explain yourself. What do you mean the queen is dead? I just saw her this morning." Lyford demanded, not noticing the smirk that quickly crossed Armen's face before it was buried.

"I mean, the queen is dead. She joined me for a ride this afternoon and was thrown when a clap of thunder spooked the horse. As near as I can tell, her neck was broken. She was gone before I dismounted."

Lyford sat down hard. The shock and disbelief raced through his mind, even as he understood the words he heard. Turning to the vizier, he didn't know which question to ask, landing on awkward. "What do I do now? We have four babies. We have

Twelve

the amendment for the merger that remains incomplete. What do I do? What do I do?" He asked rapidly as panic set in.

Armen took a steadying breath before responding. Everything was playing out exactly as he had planned. "My king, as for the children, we will have to examine our options. The amendment however. There was no stipulation that predicated what would be upon the death of the queen should she pass before time, or completion. As such, I believe you have the balance of the thirty years to secure an heir."

Lyford sat back, his face a blank canvas for every emotion as it passed. "How do I have an heir now with no queen?" He muttered to himself, but loudly enough for Armen to hear.

Armen whispered his response so as not to startle Lyford further. "You get another queen."

Quiet or not, the answer jolted Lyford. "What do you mean, get another queen?! I don't want another queen. I didn't want the one I had to begin with."

"I'm afraid, as with the first, you really have no choice. With the merger, you have to produce an heir to ascend, or surrender your kingdom."

"What have you done?!" Lyford shouted at Armen. "You set this up. You told me it would be the best way to grow my kingdom. It would have been…" His rage trailed off to incoherent mutterings.

"I advised you the best way to retain what was rightfully yours, and to protect those who put their trust in your family. Nothing more. Nothing less." Armen admonished. "All of it is still within your ability. You need a new queen, and you need to produce a male offspring. Surely that small sacrifice is manageable."

"Says you. You aren't the one being forced into another marriage of duty." Lyford challenged, pausing before continuing as a thought occurred to him. "Do you even have a wife? Do you know what it's like? Did you get to marry for love, or responsibility? You have no idea what you're asking me."

Armen's face flashed with rage. "I married the kingdom when I became vizier. Anything, or anyone, I wanted, moved beyond my grasp when I accepted the position. I know exactly what I'm asking you. I'm asking you to think of someone other than yourself."

Lyford pushed back his chair, rose, and left. He had never considered Armen's position the way it had just been described. He wanted to have an equally impassioned response, but short the words, he opted to escape.

Once again, his rage drove him to his hiding spot beyond the tapestry. This time, Bryn was nowhere in sight. Sitting, staring at the back side of the woven scene, he processed the news. Grace had certainly never been his choice. She had endured him, his demands, and the burden that the merger had placed on both of

Twelve

them. To now, he had never been willing to see it. What would he tell their daughters when they were older? He knew the truth without having to say it aloud. He wouldn't.

Word was sent to the Coeur d'Alene detailing Grace's death. Leopold arrived soon after. "Her mother and I would like to take her home." He began as soon as he was seated.

"We can arrange that." Armen answered before Lyford could speak.

"And the children?"

"We would be open to them sharing time between both households." Armen again spoke.

"While we would like to ask for more, we do recognize and appreciate that you are their father." He addressed Lyford. "Though, it is our understanding that you have little to do with them."

Lyford wanted to deny it, but couldn't. He wanted to agree to more, even go so far as letting the girls go completely, but he opted not to. Following Armen's advice that once gone, the merger would likely go as well, if not be enforced to require him to surrender his kingdom altogether, he defended a claim of lineage he didn't want to make. "Yes. I am their father. As such, their place is with me, even without their mother. I am willing to allow them to spend time with you, but with respect to our relationships. They are my children. How I interact with them, or raise them, is a matter of my household, not yours."

"As you wish. I will not interfere, yet." Leopold cautioned.

Armen perked up at the comment. "Yet? Are you still speaking with regards to the children? Or to the merger? They are significantly different details."

"As you have brought it up, perhaps we should speak of the merger. We agreed to bring our kingdoms together under one house. The death of our daughter, changes things."

Armen swung his arm out across Lyford's chest to hold his reply, speaking on his behalf instead. "It does. And, it doesn't." He began. "The amendment was conditional upon the birth of a son to ascend over both kingdoms, or upon the completion of thirty years. There was no distinction made for what would happen in the event of death. Grace's death was an accident, though even if she had passed from natural causes, or perhaps in childbirth, it would have been an unforeseen, unfortunate, and unaccounted for circumstance. What happens now, is either the agreement stands, or it has to be renegotiated. We believe, in the

Twelve

interest of the subjects of both, that letting it stand would be easier."

The patriarch of the Coeur d'Alene eased back in his chair and drew a deep breath. "I will agree, but not for long. The loss of our daughter will surely distress many. Returning them to the uncertainty they had before would not make that better. As such, I will give you one year. One year to find a new queen.

If you," he turned to address Lyford directly, "have not remarried, and consummated your new marriage by then, the merger of our lands will be severed. And, your new bride will have to take on care for my daughter's girls. I will accept nothing less." He turned to his attendant. "Write it down. I'll sign it and seal it."

Lyford's head was reeling. One year. It could be the longest or shortest in many. He glanced sideways to Armen who nodded. "That is acceptable." Armen acknowledged. "One year, and with his new union," he head canted to Lyford, "the merger agreement remains for the duration of the thirty years. Add that to what is written, and he too will sign it."

"Done."

DUTY

Eleven months and fifteen days later, Lyford wed a new queen. It was nearly all Armen could do to get the reticent king down the proverbial aisle once a suitable woman was found. The patriarch of the Coeur d'Alene was present as a witness to ensure the binding was to the letter of the agreement. He was biased against her of course, but noticed the new bride, Ava, smiled brightly at Lyford as their nuptials were recited. He tried to hope.

He left after the traditional hanging of the linens. He would have to allow the amendment to stand now. Only Armen was smiling, but he knew something no one else knew.

Ava was the illegitimate offspring of a Dukes dalliance with his mistress. As the Duchess had yet to have children of her own, she had accepted the child, but upon bearing sons of her own, efforts had been made to marry the girl off quietly. She was

Twelve

expendable. Lyford's circumstances provided the perfect solution to the situation.

Armen and the Duke had negotiated in secret. She would have three chances to bear a son. If she also failed to produce an heir to the throne, her life would be forfeit, solving the issue once and for all. If she birthed a son, the Duke and his wife's status would be elevated. Lyford was not aware of the bargain, only that she was his only option as time nearly ran out.

Ava gave birth to a daughter within the first year. As with his first four children, Lyford wanted little to do with Camden. When twins Layla and Kayla arrived a short year later, Lyford was nearly inconsolable.

Armen settled back to watch, waiting for the next attempt. He was still hoping that an heir was coming. But, he was a realist. If Lyford and Ava produced another girl, he would act according to the agreement he had made. It was unfathomable to him that there had not been a male child in the mix yet.

When Ava came up pregnant again, the castle was frenzied. She was larger than either of the previous pregnancies quickly. Speculation was rampant that she would have another multiple birth. Perhaps it would be sons. The entire kingdom awaited the delivery.

Lyford could not have felt the leveling blow any harder. Ava delivered in the early morning hours. The wait was excruciating. Before long he'd heard the two distinctly different cries, praying silently that one was a boy. They weren't. Destry and Dana were nearly identical girls in every way. The only noticeable difference was the tone of their cries.

Armen didn't wait long. Before Ava had even recovered, he acted. Unlike with Grace, as the bargain was unknown to everyone else, he acted himself. Creeping into her chambers under the cloak of night, he should have been quieter. Ava woke abruptly, jumped from the bed, and attempted to flee. Reaching a table, she grabbed the small Dirk from the drawer, unsheathed it, and spun to face her attacker. She lost her footing when she recognized Armen, falling awkwardly.

In the end, he didn't have to act. She fell on her blade. He recognized that she would soon suffocate on her own blood from the wound, electing to retreat and allow the eventual conclusion to come. What he didn't bargain for, was that she had enough presence of mind to name him. When Elba found Ava the following morning, it was in a pool of her own blood, with Armen's name written on her bedclothes.

Elba debated for several long moments. Should she confront Armen? No, if what she believed he had done was true, she needed to do everything she could to protect the girls. She should go to Lyford, but Armen controlled him. A realization struck as to what the actual dynamic potentially could be as she debated. If Armen was actually in control of the kingdom, and Lyford was only a figurehead, the arrival of a son could well mean that Lyford was disposable too. She needed to be careful.

She couldn't help the next question that came to mind, *what about Grace?* Had she actually fallen from a horse and died accidentally? Or, was there something more nefarious at play? Elba had serious misgivings about the official story. But, with no way to prove what she thought, she would need to bide her time and be watchful. She hated to do it, but she slopped some blood from the pool over the letters that spelled out Armen's name. She knew, but she could not share what she knew just yet.

Elba summoned the king. He arrived with Armen in tow a short time later. Judging by the reactions, she would wager Lyford had no idea, though he was not significantly distraught over the death, more so that someone had been inside to commit the atrocity. Armen on the other hand, was peculiarly calm. Elba watched his reaction from the corner of her eye, nearly certain she caught a glimpse of a smirk before he turned away. It was not actual confirmation, but it might be as close as she would get.

The castle was searched, but no one was found within who should not have been there. The small Dirk was easily determined to have been the instrument, but as it had lodged where she fell on it, and her hand had fallen away, there remained uncertainty as to whom had actually killed Ava. The entire residence was unsettled for many weeks following.

Lyford's mysterious disappearances became more frequent. Only Elba had managed to ascertain where he was hiding. The tapestry askew, she stopped to peer beyond it, finding him sleeping in the

Twelve

alcove. Judging by the view, she had a fairly good idea why he chose the spot. It would be another secret she would keep, for now.

TRUTHS

Over the next few years, Elba became adept at eavesdropping. Though it was never shared with the rest of the castle or the kingdom, she knew that the merger amendment was intact, though Lyford had yet to take another queen. Somehow, the condition had been mitigated before he wed Ava. They had until the conclusion of the thirty years for it to be broken if a male heir was not born to the House of Rousseau.

She also knew from a conversation between members of the guard, that Grace's death was not purely an accident. What she didn't know, was if Lyford was a party to it. She learned definitively that Armen had given the order, but she did not know the king's role. Grace had in fact been thrown, but she had not died from that. It had only been a slight of hand trick to cover her murder. Elba wanted desperately to reach out to Leopold,

Twelve

but overheard conversations would prove nothing. And, the deal was set and sealed. There was little she could do to unbind the parties. She would have to continue hiding in plain sight. She too had a role to play, and promises to keep, to Grace and to her father…protect the girls.

The next conversation Elba overheard was between Lyford and Armen.

"No, you don't have to do it today, but you do need to do it. There is no way to produce a legal heir without a queen. It simply isn't an option." Armen was chastising the king.

"Do you believe I don't know that? I do know that. The problem isn't that. The problem is that I am not willing to wed, and bed, another woman of your choosing because of their stature. We've tried that. Twice, as a matter of fact. This time, I'm doing what I want to do. Maybe, just this once, I can be happy for a change. Maybe that's what is required to produce a son. We've seen what me doing my duty results in." Lyford spat back.

Armen growled back. "Do what you will. Maybe the third time is the trick. I don't know. I don't care. You need a son. Short of figuring out how to grow one, you need a wife for that. So, make it happen."

"Fine!" Lyford shouted before turning and stomping off.

"Fine." Armen answered just before the door slammed shut.

Finding Lyford would be simple enough. He was agitated. Which meant, he would likely be hiding behind the tapestry, watching Bryn across the courtyard in the kitchens. What Elba was interested in, was to find out what Armen would do next. Her patience was rewarded.

"He is nearly as stubborn as his father." Armen addressed a member of the guard whom Elba had not noticed enter.

Peeking around the corner, she was not surprised to see it was one of the ones she had overheard below the windows talking about Grace. She already knew that Armen had given that order, what else was he willing to do? She didn't have to wait long.

"Perhaps." The guard replied. "Then again, his father had a son."

"I am well aware of his father's son. For ten years I waited for that boy to be old enough to legally be anointed. He was difficult then too. I'm not certain I can suffer him another ten years if he does finally ever have an heir while we wait for that one to come of age and be old enough." Armen groused, not lifting his eyes from the roles of parchment across the table.

"Do you believe there is another choice?"

"That will depend on when, and if, he has a son. The thirty years have a set expiration. If he has a son and the timeline expires, there is little reason to wait. It will all be foregone conclusion at that point. My concern is if he continues to have daughters. The thirty years could expire and we will lose everything. Everything I have built while he, and his father before him, thought they were in charge."

"What do you propose to do?"

Armen ran a hand through his hair. "Perhaps it is time to give him what he wants. I happen to know he is quite fond of one of the kitchen staff women. A female in his bed he actually wants might make him more easily manipulated."

The guard chortled loudly. "I know I'm easier to manipulate by a woman in my bed. If she is wild and wonton, the better."

Armen glared flatly. "I'm not suggesting for a moment that we bring in another to our arrangement. The chances are just as good that she would spill everything to him over pillow talk. No, I only mean to say that if he is content otherwise, he will be less difficult to deal with on other fronts. Or, he may have little interest in the other fronts at all, which would make things exponentially easier. Having him trifling about is a daily exhaustion."

"I see what you mean." The guard nodded. "Keep him happy, and distracted."

"Exactly."

"How will you manage it?" The guard asked belatedly.

Armen's grin was menacing. "I believe I already have. Lyford believes he has taken a stance, demanding that he should not take a wife that isn't of his choosing this time." He shrugged. "Who do you think he'll choose?"

"So that whole conversation was a set up?"

"When have you ever heard me say I don't care? I manage every nuance down to the smallest detail. The only piece of this entire thing that I haven't, only because I can't is the gender of his offspring."

Elba turned, tiptoeing away as quickly and quietly as she could manage. She had heard more than enough. Lyford was being managed by his vizier, and he didn't have the slightest clue. Or, if he had a clue, he was doing nothing to preempt it. Somehow, she couldn't decide which was worse.

Reaching her rooms, she gathered the girls and took them outside to play and get fresh air. She needed time to think. And, she needed some place to do that where if she muttered to herself, she would know if anyone was near by listening. More and more, she was coming to realize that the castle had ears.

Bridegroom

It was Lyford's turn to grin as the nuptials were spoken. He finally stood opposite, holding hands with, and reciting vows, to Bryn. Their courtship had lingered, much to the angst of many. Neither of them were getting any younger.

The ceremony itself was attended by family and a few others. Bryn had insisted on Lyford's daughters participating with them. If they were going to be a family, they needed to start from the beginning. Nine tiny bridesmaids stood with them as they exchanged the words that would bind them together.

For all of a moment, Elba almost believed that there was a happily ever after coming for the small princess's. It was only for a moment. After the ceremony, once the newlyweds were ensconced in their quarters, they seldom emerged for anyone, or anything. Elba knew that Armen was pleased by the development, as it gave him free reign for his alternative plans. For the girls however, it left them where they had always been, in Elba's care, under her watchful gaze, and clinging to her for affection. Unable to have children of her own, it was almost enough.

Before long, Elba was summoned to attend Bryn. Though she could try to deny it, or name it as any other malady, she knew without much doubt that the new queen was with child. "I believe you're pregnant."

"So soon? I thought there would be more time." Bryn countered.

"More time? More time for what?" Elba inquired, reaching for the bucket as Bryn lurched again.

"Just more time. He was my only friend when we were little. That all changed when his parents died. I lost him. I lost him to two different wives, and multiple children, and I finally got him back. I just wanted time." Bryn answered after wiping her face and wetting her tongue with a cloth.

"But what of the girls? I understand that you want time. But, what about them? He's their father. Yet, they've gotten no time."

"They are young. They won't remember." Bryn replied carelessly.

Elba had almost been willing to give her the benefit of the doubt, hoping that she would be a better parent than their actual father, but it seemed it was not to be. "As you yourself have

Twelve

discovered, time is fleeting. And it can be taken from you in the blink of an eye. The older ones remember already. They are not so young as you would hope them to be."

"They will have to wait. If I am, as you suggest, I don't believe they will be Lyford's focus now any more than they have been up to now."

Something inside Elba snapped. She heard it, recognized it, muffled it, and temporarily buried it. She had nine charges who needed her. Obviously, that was not going to change.

Bryn's late evening scream shook the castle walls. Unlike any birth before it, Lyford was present as she struggled through labor. Elba was seething, but bit back her snarky comments with the next thundering wail.

"You have to relax." She coached half-heartedly.

"That's easy for you to say." Bryn snapped. "You are not the one whose insides are trying to come out, with claws, on fire."

Elba did her best to calm her voice, though she could not take the clip from her words. "In case you've forgotten, I've done this a time or two. You need to relax, or this will be more difficult than it needs to be. Right now, the baby is backwards and you are too locked down for me to fix it. And, I promise, they don't have claws, nor are they on fire."

Elba's irritation took on a new dimension when Lyford intervened. "Bryn honey, if she says you need to relax, you need to relax. Look at me. Just look at me, and breathe. We can do this. You and me, together."

It still took some time, and some finagling, but eventually Bryn relaxed enough for Elba to turn the baby to proper presentation. Sadly, it was too little, too late. The boy was born still. Elba worked quickly to swaddle the child, handing it to the parents. She could not risk revealing her emotional response to the situation. A part of her was celebrating that the would-be heir would not be. She knew she could not let that be known, or seen, or she would jeopardize her station. The girls needed her now more than ever.

Twelve

Lyford and Bryn were absent from view for months. Elba couldn't help but hear the loud sobbing from their quarters. The loss hit them hard, but she knew Armen was getting anxious. There had been more than one conversation about the need for the couple to try again. Getting them to do so, was a component to the equation that he could not figure out how to manipulate yet.

When the couple finally emerged, Armen and everyone else learned that manipulating the equation would not be necessary. Bryn was likely pregnant again. Elba was charged with seeing her through the pregnancy successfully. Elba was less than elated.

"What about the girls? Who will be seeing to them if I am seeing to her?" She challenged as calmly as she could manage.

"I'm sure we can find someone." Lyford countered.

Elba felt the rage bubble up. If she had to see to Bryn, it would be on her terms. There was no way she was willing to let the children's care fall to anyone else at this point. "Then move her to the room on the far side of the nursery and I will do both. The girls don't know that many people, and none have had any type of consistent contact, or care for them. If you wish me to watch over Bryn, then this is how it will be done."

"She needs to be your first priority." Lyford insisted.

"They all need to be my first priority. As the nine girls are no one else's, it will have to be good enough that they are equal." Elba answered between clenched teeth.

"Done." Armen interjected, concluding the debate. "We will have her moved before nightfall."

TWELVE

Elba struggled to keep up with ten charges. As the pregnancy progressed, Bryn became more demanding day by day. Added to the challenge was Lyford's constant meddling, and unwanted instructions as to how things should be done, or when. Just past the halfway point, the queen was doing nothing for herself anymore.

By the time she delivered, Elba was almost willing to throw her hat in the ring with Armen. If another day passed as it had been for the recent months, Elba was likely to eliminate Bryn herself. As it was, the bloodied show arrived, and as expected, the queen demanded assistance. Elba was in the midst of diaper changes when it happened, with no one nearby to complete the task. Her delay was rebuked when she arrived. "Aren't you supposed to come when I call for you?" Bryn charged.

Elba drew a deep breath and collected herself before speaking. "Yes, that is what is supposed to happen. One of the twins having a blowout all over the table wasn't a factor that was considered when that edict was set. I elected to clean up first so as not to contaminate you. I thought that would be your preference. Next time, I will come in soiled." She finished with a bright smile.

Bryn scowled. "That will hardly be necessary."

"What do you need?" Elba finally asked.

Bryn produced the evidence that labor was beginning. "This."

"I'll make the necessary preparations." Elba replied before turning to leave.

"But first, get Lyford. He wants to be here for this." Bryn added.

"As you wish." She said brightly, saving the muttering and cursing until she was beyond the door.

Twelve

Lyford was nowhere to be found. Elba debated sending another to find him, deciding against it when Bryn screamed. "It's coming."

Racing in, she found Bryn fully contorted, trying to push. "Ease back. Give me just a minute." Elba instructed, getting her into position.

"I have to push. I have to push now."

The head was crowning and there was no time to delay. "Go ahead, push."

A baby girl emerged abruptly, her leg tangled with what had to be another baby. Working quickly, Elba swaddled the first and set it aside, reaching for the second.

"Where's Lyford?" Bryn cried.

"I couldn't find him, and you screamed. You need to concentrate. I'm sure everyone in the castle knows you are in labor by now. He will come as soon as he can, but I need you to help now. Focus."

"I need him."

Elba was distracted by the large amount of blood that was being delivered with the second child. Something was wrong. Working quickly, she delivered the second child, another girl, all the while listening to Bryn cry for Lyford who had not arrived.

Setting the second girl next to her mother, Elba tried to discover the source of the bleeding. What she found was a third infant preparing to deliver. "Bryn, I need you to breathe, and calm down. There's another baby that I need to get out before we can take care of you."

"Another baby? How can there be another baby?"

"We will discuss how that works later, right now, we need to get them out." Elba chastised as she worked.

Before the third baby could be delivered, Bryn slumped. The choices were not good, and worse. She could not save Bryn until the third baby was out. It was going to be difficult to get the third baby out without Bryn's assistance. With Grace in the forefront of her mind, she made a split-second decision. It really wasn't a choice, there was only one way to proceed. She had to deliver the child.

Screaming like a banshee, Elba delivered Bryn and Lyford's son. Not stopping to consider her actions, she swaddled the child quickly and set him aside, returning her attention to the mother. Judging by the volume of blood, the shallow respirations, and the incoherent mutterings, she was not long for this world.

Lyford finally arrived. Elba was teetering on the verge of collapse. "What's happened? Why isn't she more alert?" He absently noticed the three bundles. "Three? She had three?"

"Yes, she had three, and it may have been more than she could do. I have been trying to get the bleeding to stop, but I can't. Her breathing has shallowed, and her awareness is dim."

"Why didn't you save her first? I have plenty of daughters. You should have saved her."

Twelve

Elba verbally slapped him. "I couldn't save her until they were out. She couldn't help with the third, so it took longer. I'm doing everything that I can."

"You're not doing enough."

"Take over then if you think you can do better." She snapped.

"I don't know what to do."

"Then stay out of my way and let me try. I'm doing the best that I can." Elba chastised, trying to calm herself.

Bryn rallied, but only for a moment. "Lyford, you came."

"I'm here, love. I'm here."

"We have…" Bryn began, but drifted off.

Lyford looked at the three bundles, saw the blankets tinged pink from all the blood, and jumped to the wrong conclusion. "I know. I see. More girls."

Elba understood his mistake, but did not stop to correct him. Bryn tried, but was gone before she could finish. "No… We h…"

Elba continued working, though she knew at that point Bryn was already gone. It was only a show for Lyford. Eventually, Lyford knew it too. "Just take the babies and leave me with her." He dismissed when the truth became undeniable.

Elba picked up the babies, tucking the boy in close, and retreated to the nursery. She considered her options as she went. She could, based on what she understood of Armen's plan, reveal the son and potentially rid all the girls of their father, or she could somehow secret his identity, and leave the future to play out. She decided on the latter.

When Lyford had not shown any interest in meeting the three newest children, Elba took it upon herself to name them. Shara, Erin, and Devlin became the latest Rousseau children, bringing the total to twelve.

ESCAPE

Over a year later, Lyford's depression would have been moving to Elba if he had shown a fraction of it for either of his other wives. Elba knew that Bryn was his only love. She'd known since before Grace's death. It enraged her over and over again to see it so predominantly on display now. The children were growing, and could see it as well. Most everyone avoided him when possible. Only Armen seemed to take issue and react. "Grieve and move on, Lyford."

"It will take as long as it will take. I am well aware of your concerns. They will have to wait." Lyford snapped back uncharacteristically.

Elba was just beyond the door, hearing the conversation easily. She didn't want to hear anymore, as it would not be any different than the dozens of others that had already been had.

She knocked tentatively to stop it, waiting to be acknowledged before entering. "What do you want?" Lyford challenged.

"A plan." Elba stated simply.

"What kind of a plan?" Armen queried, his head tipped in curiosity.

"For the girls…" Elba replied, standing firm but trying to keep her tone level. "There are twelve of them now, and many are of an age where they need more guidance than I can provide as a nursemaid. They will be young ladies before we can blink. Some formal education is in order for the older ones, and perhaps for the younger ones too."

"The triplets are barely a year old." Lyford scoffed. "They hardly need education."

Elba shook her head gently. "The triplets were not at the forefront of my thoughts."

Lyford waved her off, physically dismissing her without words. Armen actually interjected. "What do you suggest?"

"I suggest that we start looking."

Dancing Shoes

A dozen years later, Elba and the twelve were tucked safely away across the northeastern border. They had been for many years already. The boarding school was exactly what Elba had hoped for. By the time they arrived, each of the children got attention to meet their individual needs, but away from classes, they were able to remain together as a family, with Elba as their primary caretaker.

The only exception to the more individualized classes that the children got, was the time spent in dance lessons. It had become a thorn in their fathers hide. Each time the children reached out to him, or more exactly, the only time they reached out to him, was for new dance shoes. It was not lost on Elba that they were giving back to him in equal proportion to what he had given them. He could not see it that way, but anyone who had known of their circumstances, couldn't miss the irony.

Through the years, Elba was there. In many ways she was more their mother than anything. She ached to reveal her true relationship, but withheld it, knowing that she could not do so for all, and as such, she became to all of them in equal measure. Through bumps and bruises, blisters and broken toes, she was there to kiss the wounds, and mend the rest. She became their confidant and friend too. As new discoveries were made for places and things beyond the school, she was there to support, or to keep their secrets.

"One day, right Elba? One day he'll see me for who I am." Devlin asked innocently from her lap.

"My sweet, sweet boy, perhaps one day. But, to see you for who you are, would be to reveal what you are." She soothed.

"But I want to be this way."

"Yes love, I know. And, the choice should be yours. Unfortunately, there is great pressure for your father to have a son. I'm afraid that your choices would be gone if he found out now."

"He doesn't like girls."

"I can't answer that. I don't know if he likes boys either. He needs a son. That means a boy. I don't know if it has anything to do with what he likes, or wants, or anything else."

Twelve

"So what you're saying... Is that a boy, who likes other boys, and prefers to dress like a girl, would not be good."

"Devlin, who you are is good, no matter how you are. You are a brilliant young man, with the whole world to explore. Once you are older, no one will have a say. Until then, for the next few years, at least until you come of age, it would be better left this way." Elba counseled.

Devlin and his twin sisters were on the cusp of thirteen. They only had to get through a few more years before legally, no one could force them to do, or be anything else. Their eldest sister, Aislyn, was already there. She was having different growing pains.

As if thinking of her drew her to the room, Aislyn appeared. She tousled Devlin's hair as she spoke to Elba. "I have some friends I'd like to hang out with." She began carefully. "Would that be all right?"

Elba didn't miss the odd tone. "Why do you ask it like that?"

"No reason. I mean, I know I can go, legally I'm able, I'm just trying to figure out when I still need to ask, and when I don't."

"Have fun then." Elba replied. "I appreciate your consideration. Don't be too late."

Aislyn was off without another word.

Savannah Verte

Several years later, Elba was keeping a monumental secret. All of the children had come of age. She did not have the legal right to deny them, but she was not a party to the decision, or in attendance as the choices were made. All twelve, one by one, had found their way to the stage. Logan's Lost Lounge was a myth to anyone who had never been there. Complete with showgirls, bright lights, big costumes, and more, it was exactly the sort of place no one would look for twelve princesses, or eleven princesses and one very effeminate prince.

As Lyford had never come to visit, only demanding the children make an appearance at the castle every so often, he was none the wiser. The only thing that potentially could have tipped him off was the shoe budget. Requests for money, or anything else, had ceased. Even that, he was not interested in enough to pay attention, or so Elba believed.

It was only when Devlin joined the group that Elba agreed to see the club finally.

Twelve

"Please Elba. Please come. I am exactly who I'm supposed to be there. I'm free. I need you to see it." Devlin pleaded.

"One time. One time now that you are old enough, and able to make the choice. This way, I can state absolutely that I did not have a role in this choice." She acquiesced. "I had to keep my distance while you three were still coming of age."

When she walked in, she was taken back by the scene. Everything about the club was erogenous. Even the stage was phallic. A long runway jutted out into the club, subdividing the floor cleanly in two. Twin small arcs flanked it on one end where it intersected with the curtain. And, the whole stage was studded through with polished, shiny poles. If she'd had any notion of what to expect by the condition the girls had returned in night after night, she still never would have imagined this.

Elba had combed more than her share of small glittery bits out of hair, and plucked feathers in every color she could think of from other clothes. She, and others, had nearly tumbled multiple times stepping on, and sliding over renegade beads that were littered across the floor. What these combinations amounted to, she hadn't paused to give much thought to. Seeing the lounge in person, she wasn't sure she was ready to know.

Making her way to a table, she was nearly blinded by any number of the multiple spotlights, all of them focused on the audience. She didn't understand that until Raven took the stage and they turned. Dressed in a costume that made her look like she was wearing an exotic bird, the lights all turned, focusing exclusively on her as she cleared the curtain.

Elba was busily watching Raven dance. Her movements were evocative and made Elba blush. She was so captivated by her movements, it wasn't until nearly all of the girls had joined Raven onstage that Elba noticed there was anyone else on stage. Before long, twelve dancers were moving across the stage with and around one another. They were between the poles, or just as easily on them in any number of contorted poses. Elba couldn't keep track.

When she finally spotted Devlin, she was overcome. He looked just like the others. Even knowing he was not a female, to look at him, she could not tell. He was beautiful. More than that, he was beaming. Elba spent the rest of the evening paying close attention. She knew she would not be returning, but when asked, she would be able to honestly say what a wonderful job he had done.

MISERY

Back at the kingdom, the clock was ticking. There were only a few years left before the thirty-year deadline would lapse. Lyford had never fully recovered from the loss of his beloved Bryn. Armen was running out of options.

"What if he gained a son by a mistress and married her then?" One of the guards asked.

"I don't see how we can back into that." Armen replied. "Besides, Leopold is more stalwart and stubborn then I gave him credit. I had thought by the end of the thirty years he would be gone already. I miscalculated. I firmly believe that he will outlast the amendment, if only by a day, to see it fail now."

"But why? He will have gained nothing other than more of a kingdom with no heir to rule. What if one of the princesses would marry? That's how he merged his kingdom the first time. Why not now?"

Armen was pensive. He knew that it would be a delicate negotiation, if it happened at all. But, pending nuptials might be enough to sway the equation. He would have to talk to Lyford. He hated to. He would prefer to handle it himself, but knew that wouldn't work.

The king was busy salving his wounds with any vice he could manage. Multiple mistresses had come and gone from his bedchamber, all of them unfulfilled. The lure of potentially bedding, and perhaps one day marrying the king got them there, but his lack of performance preempted return visits.

The latest in the lineup tried a second time, but left again, never to return, after Lyford called her Bryn during foreplay. She could not bring herself to be a stand-in for the dead queen. Armen pleaded with her to try again, before broaching the alternative subject with Lyford when she declined.

Twelve

"We are running out of time." Armen announced, ripping open the old wound.

"I am well aware of the time. I am also well aware that I am an older man now. What chance do you think I have of conceiving a child, never mind a son? Been there, done that. I've got a dozen daughters to show for the effort."

"Perhaps we could modify the agreement. If, we had something more to bargain with." Armen tempted.

"What exactly do you have in mind? I'm fairly certain that neither you, nor I, have anything that the Coeur d'Alene is interested in now. He is an older man than I am."

"What if one of your daughter's were to marry? Surely the idea of a coming wedding would be good news for the Coeur d'Alene. It would certainly go a long way to calm the masses on our side."

Lyford scoffed, waving Armen off with a halfhearted shrug. "How do you intend to get one of them to marry? Better yet, how do you intend to get one of them to marry, and want to return here? They've been gone for ages, and even when they come back, they are gone again before nightfall."

"They are all of age…" Armen voiced slowly. "I could marry one of them." He added, trying to sound offhand.

Lyford's head snapped up. "No. You cannot marry one of them."

"Why not?!" Armen demanded before recovering his temper.

"Because they align you with me. You see how much they want to spend time with me. There is no way that an engagement to you would draw any of them back."

Armen was surprised by the logic of the response, his knee-jerk reaction being far different for what he believed the reason was. "Okay, then what's option number two?"

"I don't know."

"Then I suggest that we try option number one. The time it will take to get them to return, convince them, even one of them, and proposition the Coeur d'Alene with the news, will take us to the precipice of the mergers failure date."

HOME

The summons arrived on a Monday.

> *By order of King Lyford Rousseau, your presence is required for the announcement of a marriage. All parties here in will attend.*
> *Aislyn, Feraut, Evelyn, Raven, Camden, Layla, Kayla, Destry, Dana, Shara, Erin, & Devlin.*

Elba read the missive, nodded to the courier, and retreated. "A marriage?" She wondered aloud. "Who is he marrying this time?"

Once everyone had gathered, Elba read the notice aloud. Objections came from all directions.

"Will attend? Awful presumptuous."

"Marriage? Who's getting married?"

"Required? Since when does he have enough of anything to do with us to make requirements?"

"Hush. Hush." Elba said loudly, pumping her open palms downward. "You are still the wards of his kingdom. Legally, you are adults, and as such, can make your case to decline, though it may be a more difficult situation than to just be present."

"We will go, as long as you are with us." Camden finally announced after the conversation lulled.

Elba grinned broadly. "Legally adult or not, I would not have it any other way than to be by your side."

They agreed to set off in the morning at first light. Perhaps, they could get it over with, be gone, and be back home again, by nightfall.

"Okay, you've got us here. What's the announcement? Who's getting married?" Dana cut to the chase as soon as they were collectively in audience with their father.

Twelve

"And here I had thought that you might have learned some manners." He retorted sharply.

"We have learned plenty. School has nothing to do with our manners toward you. We are simply returning that which we received." Evelyn clipped. "You required our attendance, we are attending."

If Lyford had thought this would go quickly, well, or easily, he buried those hopes quickly. "As you may or may not know, many years ago, nearly thirty years ago to be precise, an agreement was made with the kingdom of the Coeur d'Alene across the northern border. The agreement was that our kingdoms would be merged under one house. The stipulation to the continued alignment of our subjects, was that a son would one day assume the throne over both."

"That's why there are so many of us?" Kayla interrupted. "You wanted a boy?"

Lyford exhaled forcefully. "Yes, that's true. However, as I have daughters, we are hopeful to salvage the union of our kingdoms by way of a marriage. With this in mind, Armen, my trusted vizier, has agreed to wed…"

Raven shot up from her seat. "Armen is not an heir to this throne."

Lyford swallowed hard, glanced sideways to Armen, and looked back to his daughters. "No, he is not. But, all of you are." He stated, letting the implication hang.

"Absolutely not!" Elba jumped up to stand in front of the rest.

"Elba, your presence was not requested, nor is it required. You have no say in this matter." Armen scolded before Lyford could speak.

"I have been here since the first of these children were born. I have been the one who swaddled, bathed, dressed, taught, and cared for each of them since the day of their births. Not only that, but I will absolutely do whatever is necessary to prevent any of them from marrying you." She spat back.

Lyford could follow the logic to a point, but could not make the jump to understand why she would protest so earnestly. "What's wrong with him?" He challenged. "He has cared for this kingdom since before I was born. There is no more loyal subject in the land."

Elba snapped. Long buried secrets were coming out and she voluntarily became the mouthpiece, even knowing the children were listening. They needed to hear it too. It had been too long. "Is that what you think? Ask him how Ava died? Ask him why she wore his name in blood across her gown by her own hand when she could do nothing else. Go ahead, ask him!" She challenged as Armen flushed and Lyford blanched.

"Ask him how Grace died. You've lived in denial. I've lived in the shadows, where no one thought to guard their words. I've heard them talking. I know he was responsible. Ask him why

Twelve

each of your wives only got three chances to produce a son. I'd be willing to bet he knows how your parents died too." Elba shouted before she could stop herself.

Every jaw in the room was slack except for Armen and his guard's whose hand darted to the hilt of his sidearm. Elba wasn't finished yet. "You wrapped yourself in the cloak of duty, all the while denying your children. They will not marry him. If you are half the king you want everyone to believe, you won't keep him now knowing the truth."

"Take her into custody." Armen directed the guard.

"Do not!" Lyford interjected, grabbing the small Dirk from his boot and setting it along Armen's throat. "Tell me. Tell me she lies." He said a breath away from Armen's face.

"She is a servant. You would take her word?"

"That isn't a denial."

"No. It isn't."

The scuffle was quick, surprising everyone. In the fracas, several things happened simultaneously. Armen's guard was too slow, the king, for once in his life, was too fast, and no one moved to intervene. When it was done, Armen laid bleeding out on the floor, his guard trying to stem the flow, but losing by the moment with the king standing over them both. "So, it's true."

"Believe what you want. The truths that I know will never be yours now." Armen rasped, gasping for breath.

"Take them with you. You won't need them where you're going and they've done no good here." Lyford turned back to his children. "I didn't know."

"Sadly," Aislyn spoke up, "what you did or didn't know, doesn't matter now. What's done is done."

Staring at the group, he belatedly noticed that several of them had bruises in different stages of healing. For as many pair that he had bought through the ages, he noticed too that all of their shoes were worn nearly through. For a formal announcement, they had come to the castle dressed as little more than peasants.

"I know I can't ask it, but it would still be best if one of you were to marry." Lyford said. He knew he was already defeated, the last-ditch effort was all he had left.

"What happens if none of us marry?" Devlin queried in an awkward falsetto.

Lyford shrugged. It took him a moment to answer as he belatedly noticed that Devlin's hair was pink. "Then the agreement expires and our kingdom falls to the Coeur d'Alene."

Destry snorted. "You've married before. Guess you better try again. It's your kingdom to lose. We don't want it."

Lyford slumped. Nothing more was said on the subject. Try as he might, he knew he did not have the words, or the right, to ask for more, or again. He watched as they turned collectively and left with Elba, truly the one person who had ever been there

Twelve

for them. He couldn't blame them for it, it was all they knew. And, it was all his fault.

CHANGES

The team at the boarding house had been more than accommodating. While technically there was no set requirement that anyone move out immediately upon passing their final courses, the twelve and Elba had lingered far longer than most. Several years longer in fact. Because of the unique situation, they had all been allowed to stay together, but it was becoming awkward. "We need to move on. All of you are well beyond the age of anyone else here." Elba commented offhand one evening.

"Actually," Aislyn chimed in brightly, "we found somewhere. We just needed a little time to make it all work out."

Elba eyed her, choosing her next words carefully. "By that, I would take it to mean that you will not be returning to the castle."

Twelve

"No. We won't. But, we understand if you are required to. We hope that you will come with us instead though." Erin tempted.

"As long as you will have me, I will be where you are."

"Great!" Kayla dashed around the end of the table to hug Elba fiercely. "We want you to see it, tomorrow."

"Tomorrow?"

"Yes, tomorrow." Layla interjected. "We are not completely oblivious. We heard the headmistress speak to you again the other day. We knew we were out of time."

"Tomorrow it is then."

Their residence was not the only thing changing. Logan's Lost Lounge was under construction, which made the timing nearly ideal. New rooms were being added, and as such, the club was operating minimally. It was the perfect time to move, though moving didn't take nearly as long as the renovations.

Elba did not join them for their return trip to the lounge. She had gone once, and once was enough for her. She did not approve, nor disapprove, but she didn't need to bear witness repeatedly.

Nerissa, the club manager showed them around upon their return. The changes were extravagant. Themed rooms had been added on both sides of the main floor. The rules however, remained the same, no touching, at least not from the patrons.

The first room they saw was covered in silver and mirrors. It was high profile. Dancers in this room would be tasked with channeling the aristocracy. Several of the girls laughed. "If she only knew." One of them muttered under their breath.

The second room was equally themed in extravagance. Nearly every surface was covered in gold. It was opulent and shouted wealth. The dancers in this room would be dressed to match.

On the opposite side of the main floor was a room that was more comfortable in appearance. Chairs were scattered in pockets where patrons could enjoy a private dance, but at the same time, all dancers would be easily viewed. Prior to this, the closest interactions with patrons only happened on the main floor, which was awkward with the major stage as a focal point.

Last was a room of jewels. Diamonds, rubies, emeralds, sapphires, and others twinkled from their placements. The room itself was done in colors to match. This room had no overtone,

Twelve

but was, like the one next to it, for a more comfortable setting, while still drawing a picture of something more intimate than the main stage.

"Who goes where?" Camden asked as they returned to the main floor.

"Everyone will have opportunities to rotate through any of the rooms. No one is assigned, though some may be more comfortable than others. We would still like the twelve of you to dance together, but this would provide an opportunity for you each to showcase yourself individually as well."

"How much longer until everything is ready?" Raven asked.

"Just a few more days. I know that you have relocated. It should give you time to settle before you return. We will look for you a week from Friday."

"Perfect!" Devlin said, clapping his hands together. "I want to put some new costumes together by then too."

The base costumes are started and waiting in your dressing rooms." Nerissa giggled. "You are welcome to personalize, so long as they stay to the themes."

The conversation erupted to discussions of jewels, feathers, beads, glitter, and most importantly, new shoes. It wasn't a contest, but it was going to be one of sorts. Each of them had different ideas about how to showcase themselves as individuals, and none were wasting a moment.

Savannah Verte

Within time things took on a new routine. Each of the Rousseau twelve had turns in the new rooms, but they all came together for their showcase on the main stage each night. They each had gained dedicated audiences as well. Suitors lined up outside the lounge night after night to see them dance, and waited for turns in the chairs for private entertainment. Proposals were common, but none ever accepted. The twelve were enjoying their freedom too well to consider giving it up. Eventually, they came to be known as the Twelve Dancing Princesses, a moniker they laughed about often.

NEW PLAN

Lyford's melancholy drove deeper toward depression. His past cropped up to greet him as soon as he opened his eyes. He soon accepted that it was not a nightmare, but his reality. Before long, it found him before his eyes even opened. He knew too well that his time was nearly up, and there was no potential solution on the horizon. He knew of the Lost Lounge, and it's Twelve Dancing Princesses. Even so, he had not put it together with his daughters.

He tried again to mend fences, reaching out to them with an impromptu visit. He was devastated a new to find their living arrangements sadly lacking the opulence of his castle and kingdom. They were not moved by his gesture.

He detoured from his return trip. He had spent much of the ride considering what he had seen. Left with no alternatives, he crossed back over the northern border, and went to see the only person who could alter the future. Though they had merged their kingdoms together ages before, he'd never actually made the trip before. The castle for the Coeur d'Alene was resplendent. As an uninvited guest, he waited in the foyer for audience to be granted.

"Leopold will see you." The servant announced without emotion. "This way please."

Entering the small study, Lyford was surprised to see Leopold. He remained a picture of health. Anyone seeing them together could easily assume that Lyford was the elder, and Leopold the junior. "This is a surprise." The patriarch of the Coeur d'Alene opened, snapping Lyford from his thoughts.

"It is a surprise to me too. I had not intended to come here this day."

"Oh?" Leopold quipped. "What changed?"

"I have been to see my daughters."

"That too surprises me."

"Well…" Lyford began, shifting from foot to foot.

"Why don't you sit? It seems this will be a long tale." Leopold interjected, motioning toward a chair.

Lyford sat heavily. "Once upon a time, I had thought that there was a way to still fulfill our agreement. I know now, that is not true. I accepted, and acted, upon bad advice, and the result is what it will be. They want nothing to do with me. They want nothing to do with my kingdom. And, they feel no obligation to

Twelve

the agreement we made." He leveled quickly before he could change his mind.

"So I have heard."

"Which part?" Lyford asked before he processed the actual words.

"All of it. But, I too bear some responsibility. I should have known then that you were too young. I should have known that Armen was instigating the merger agreement. Looking back, it is much clearer. At the time, it was almost divine intervention." Leopold paused. "You have daughters now, so you can appreciate the burden of needing an heir, and of the driving inclination to intervene."

Lyford drug a hand down his face. "You give me more credit than I deserve. When I heard the plan, my thought was to expand my kingdom. It had nothing to do with an heir, I presumed that would take care of itself. Even now, even if I wanted to, intervening is not an option. They have made it abundantly clear that they are in charge of their futures now. I lost that right when they were born and I walked away."

Leopold chuckled, drawing Lyford from his self-deprecation. "Forgive me if this sounds condescending. I don't mean it to be. But, welcome to the game."

"I beg your pardon?"

Leopold leaned back, rubbed his chin, and considered his next words. "At some point in our lives, each of us has to come to terms with what is real, and what is never going to be. Some of us, have the benefit of guidance to reach that point. Others, like you, don't. For all their faults, your parents were good people. With them gone, you had no one to show you the differences. Your trust was misplaced, and as such, you paid a steep price. It's a game. It's called life. Be glad that you learned it. Some never do."

Lyford stared at the elder man. His comments were not from a position of judgment, though he certainly had the right after everything that had happened. "But, I can't change it. The game has been played and I have lost."

Leopold tilted his head from side to side. "Yes, and no."

"How do you mean?"

"I mean…" Leopold grinned, "Yes, the game as you knew it has been played. And, you did indeed lose. But, because the game is part of a larger landscape called life, there is always another game to be played. The question is, will you now, or do you surrender?"

"Surrender? You mean my kingdom, sorry, our kingdom?"

"No…" Leopold laughed robustly, shaking his head. "No, I wasn't referring to that. I meant, will you stand up to participate in the game as it is being played now. You don't have to, I suppose. You haven't participated for quite a long time now. It's your choice. I'm asking if you will choose, or if you will accept the defeat as it was dealt."

Twelve

Lyford was lost. "I don't understand."

Leopold held up his hand to pause Lyford. "Let's consider my game then. I have daughters. My kingdom needed an heir. I could have decided that there was no hope, but instead, I entered into an agreement with you, to be the heir to our combined kingdoms by marriage to one of my daughters. In exchange, I got thirty years to see from a different perspective. My game was changed. Your game too, can be changed."

Lyford huffed in exasperation. "They want nothing to do with me, didn't you understand that?"

"What if it isn't through you?"

Lyford stared blankly. His mind was racing, trying to grasp the meaning, but only circling in confusion. "Again, I don't understand."

Leopold stood, paced to the fireplace and back again before speaking. "Look, the merger between our two kingdoms, at least for the next couple of years, remains in the balance. Your appearance here, while unanticipated, presents an opportunity for us to change the game. What I am suggesting, is that circumstances be manipulated in such a way so that it is their idea."

"Their idea for what?"

"To marry. To ascend. All of it."

Lyford's eyes went wide. "They want nothing to do with me now. I don't think I could bear it if the aversion changed to overt hate for manipulating them."

Leopold nodded as he sat back down. "I understand. It is a delicate thing. I think it can be done in such a way that they would never know."

"This was a mistake..." Lyford began as he started to rise.

"No. This is the first that you have tried to be king, to be responsible, to be their parent. Your job is not for them to like you, it is for you to put them in a position to become more than they are. You've never done that. It's high time."

"Tell me how." Lyford finally acquiesced, still uncertain this would end well.

The balance of the evening was spent laying out plans, simple plans to drive his daughters to succeed in spite of how they felt. Multiple times, Lyford was sure it would fail. Leopold reassured him, reminding him that he also had multiple daughters, and sometimes to get them to act one way, you had to behave as if you are pushing them to act another.

Lyford felt ancient and juvenile, all at the same time before he left. He had little hope that the plan would succeed, but with no other alternatives, he agreed. The agreement between the houses, while formally would stand with the impending due date, between them now had no expiration. With so many possibilities, Leopold was certain an heir was coming.

Flies

Word spread like wildfire through the lands that any available prince who could win the heart of one of Lyford's daughters, and gain her promise of marriage, would become heir to the combined Rousseau - Coeur d'Alene kingdoms. The twelve were incensed and aghast immediately. "Who does he think he is?" Destry demanded angrily.

"He can't force this, can he?" Evelyn asked as she turned to Elba.

"I don't know." Elba answered softly. "You are his children. It could be within his purview, though it is a careless plan. He learned nothing evidently from his own mistakes."

"What do we do?" Dana asked somberly.

Aislyn laid a hand on Elba's forearm. "We rise above. If any come calling, we can be cordial, but that's all we need to be. We do not allow his desperation to dictate. Agreed?" She asked, searching the other's faces.

"Agreed." Came back nearly in unison.

In short order there seemed to be a revolving door at the household. Princes, and princes-in-waiting from kingdoms they had never heard of, arrived in droves. Each time they were cordial and hospitable, though often it made them run late. Before long, they were plying their would-be suitors with libations so as to make their escape. Unfortunately, it often left Elba with the responsibility to eject them when they woke.

On several occasions, fights erupted as the posturing at the household took on different dimensions. Those parties were asked to leave immediately. Still, there was a steady flow of interested males that came and went from the property day after day.

Under any other circumstances, they might have caved for a few of the men, but they bolstered each other day by day. They

Twelve

were determined to hold fast. If Lyford honestly believed that his plan could work, he would be sorely mistaken.

WANDERER

When the cold winter months finally ended, Devlin could take no more. "Throw open the windows and beat out the blankets. I can smell a dozen different colognes, and none of them were that good solo." He chirped too early one morning.

"Devlin! We are trying to sleep." Feraut called back drowsily.

Devlin cocked out his hip and snapped in a zigzag. "Sleep when you're dead sister. This place is disgusting. Anyone who doesn't know what is going on here would think this is a brothel for all the men that come and go."

Several pillows launched from as many beds in his general direction. He was not moved. If anything, it spurned him on further. Racing the room, just out of reach, he ran past each bed and pulled the covers, taking them with him as he went to the

Twelve

next. "You don't want your pillows, you don't need your blankets. Move it ladies, move it!"

"Devlin!!" Raven shouted as he reached her bed, jumping out to block his path. They dissolved into a heap amid fits of giggles.

"What?!" He demanded, winded from laughter. "Tell me you can stand this. It's awful. And, it stinks. Can't you smell it? If my nose had a nose it would be offended."

"Enough drama-queen." Shara interjected, grabbing her blanket from the pile and turning to head back to bed. "We know. It stinks. You can't stand it. But, we're tired. Let. Us. Sleep."

Elba appeared in the doorway as she finished. "Breakfast is ready."

Devlin sashayed over to Elba, pecked her on the cheek, and grinned. "They don't need breakfast. Evidently, they need their beauty sleep."

"Be nice."

"Oh Elba… That was nice." Devlin countered before moving past her toward the stairs.

Elba swatted back, catching his hip with her fingertips. "Don't think you're too big…" She teased.

Devlin cocked out his hip, leaning forward on a twist. "Do it again."

"I don't know who you think you're playing with. Don't tempt me."

Savannah Verte

Closer to home, wandering along the border between the Rousseau and Coeur d'Alene properties, a young man encountered a sorceress who was out in the woods. "What business do you have here?" She inquired as he neared.

"I'm only passing through." He answered, offering no other information.

"Through to where?" She queried further.

"To the home of the twelve princesses."

"Are you a prince?"

"Not exactly."

She studied him with her head cocked sideways. "How exactly does one become, not exactly, a prince?"

Figuring that he was unlikely to escape without elaboration, he elected to tell his tale, get it over with, and be able to move on toward his destination. "I am the fourth son of seven to King Hébert. Does that make me a prince? Yes. And no. My eldest brother is the prince, or…" He shrugged, "now the King."

Twelve

"So you are a prince." She grinned brightly.

"I am an outcast. There, I was a prince. Here, now, I'm just a man… A man with no kingdom, no home, and no future. As none yet have been able to sway any of the promised princesses, my shot is as good as any." He finished his tale, turning to leave.

"Perhaps I can help you." She said, stunning him.

"Why would you do that?"

"Do you know where you are?"

"Roughly."

"You are in their kingdom. Should I not want to see one of them, any of them, marry and return someday?"

"I suppose." He replied cautiously, turning back.

When he faced her, she produced a cloak. "Take this, but do not go to their home. Go to Logan's. There you will find them. Wear this to observe them first. See if any strike your fancy. The promise of wealth and a kingdom is a poor replacement for a person."

Arigany made his way to the Lost Lounge. He entered just as the twelve were performing in showcase in the main room. From beneath the cloak he stared as each one moved to the head of the stage. Each was more beautiful than the last, but when the last came, he could not look away.

It wasn't the shock of pink hair that held his attention. Nor, was it the costume. It might have been the fluid movements, but even those he could ignore. There was something about the twelfth princess that held him riveted.

Night after night he returned. And, night after night, he couldn't help but drift from room to room to wherever the one called Devlin was. She was intoxicating, but she was also something more. He was nearly certain what it was, but filled with just enough doubt. Completely infatuated, Arigany began collecting bits…costume bits that he'd notice drift down as Devlin performed.

Eventually, deep down, he knew the truth. While an extremely good female impersonation was happening before his eyes, he doubted vehemently that Devlin was a princess. But, what were the chances he would be interested in return? The act, the doting female act was convincing, but could it be real? Or, was he just that good of a showman? How could Arigany find out?

LAP DANCES

Arigany finally ditched the cloak. Determined not to act in haste, he spent the next weeks observing each of the princesses. From the room with the private alcoves, he attempted to engage them each in conversation. Sadly, while pleasant, none held his attention.

When at last he spoke to Devlin, something shifted. "You are quite limber." He said, silently chastising himself for the cliché comment.

"Call it good genes…" Devlin teased, trailing a long finger down Ari's forearm. "You look like you could be limber too."

"Not like you." Ari countered, reaching up to return the gesture. "You're beautiful."

"Hands on the chair lover." Devlin commanded, pulling back slightly.

"Is that how this works?"

Devlin waved in the air. "Works, doesn't work, doesn't matter. Those are the rules."

Ari was intrigued. "So you can touch me, but I can't touch you?" He clarified.

"That's the deal, handsome."

"Then show me what you've got." He challenged.

Unwittingly, Devlin rose to the bait. It was probably the best lap dance he had ever given. Skimming over the flesh of the handsome stranger, Devlin was lost to the sensations, and his thoughts. He'd seen this man in the club before, but with his sisters, or the other dancers. He couldn't say for sure how many times the patron had come in. He'd noticed him often, but never interacted with him up close, assuming the he just wasn't interested.

Devlin realized too late that somewhere in the middle of the dance he had crossed a line. His physical response was going to prevent him from finishing, or just might mean him finishing if he wasn't careful. Unable to do anything else, he rose, turned, and finished the dance backwards, twisting around to place a peck on the man's cheek before leaving. "That one's on me, lover." He whispered before dashing off.

Back in the dressing room, he grabbed the first of his sisters that he saw. Just his luck it was Destry. "I have a problem."

Twelve

She rolled her eyes as she responded. "I've known that for years. What do you think your problem is?"

Gesturing his hips with both hands, his problem was evident. "This."

"What did you do?" She challenged in shock.

"I did my job. I did a dance. I did…" He shrugged, "nothing out of the ordinary."

"If that's the ordinary, how is it that you still have a job as a dancing princess?" Destry challenged, grabbing Layla and Kayla to help surround Devlin. "We have a problem."

"What…" They began before they noticed. "Wow. Go big or go home, huh?"

"Very funny. What do I do?"

Raven poked her head between her sisters just then. "What do you normally do when that happens?"

Devlin rolled his eyes. "Don't make a fuss about this. This doesn't normally happen."

"Never?"

"Of course not, never! It would take an act of the Goddess to undo the precautions. I have the tightest little G-string of anyone in this club, plus a pair of booty shorts one size too small underneath the pair you can see to prevent this from happening. Yes, never!"

"Okay… Then what do you normally do when that happens and you're not wearing three layers of clothes?" Raven asked sounding irritated.

Devlin tapped his foot, slammed both fists on his hips, and shrieked incoherently. "You're going to make me say it, aren't you? This doesn't happen to me." He eyeballed her hard. "There, do you get it now?"

"Really? Who was it then? Do tell."

"Oh my Gods. Enough! Yes, really."

"Wow."

"Wow?…" Devlin countered, "Wow. Seriously? That's all you have? That's your great advice? That's all you can say? I'm in serious trouble here."

"Most of the guys in the club wouldn't say that's serious trouble. I think most of them would think it's a good thing." Layla said innocently.

"Oh really? So, you think I can just go out and continue the show as if nothing has happened? You think no one is going to notice that one of the dancing princesses has a log in her shorts? We have very different definitions of trouble."

When the giggling subsided, they all could at least acknowledge there was a problem. None of them however knew what to do about it. Aislyn finally suggested a temporary solution. "If you don't know how to deal with that, you could always go get some cold water. Maybe it will go away until later."

Twelve

"Right now I think I hate you all." Devlin muttered. "Tell Nerissa I've taken ill. I'll be back if I can, or tomorrow."

"Oh, so now we all get part of your problem." Dana moaned.

"Yes dear, it's that, or expose that we aren't what we say we are. Your choice. Log? Or lie?"

"Fine. Lie." She moaned.

Arigany saw Devlin slip from the back room. He donned the cloak and followed. He was many things, but a fool was not one of them. Long before Devlin had changed positions on him, he thought he had an answer to if Devlin would be interested in return or not. The idea kept him moving to find out. It was now or never.

A Man

Elba was fast asleep when Devlin arrived. Tiptoeing in, he worked quickly to liberate himself from the restrictive costume. The ache was excruciating. The trouble was, he had no more idea how to ease it now, than he'd had at the club. Thanks to his sisters, he was as oblivious as before.

Not wanting to wake Elba, he eased out the side door, hoping some fresh air would help alleviate his discomfort. The wind was cool, but it brought with it the scent of a man. It was one he recognized too. The too familiar ache returned to confirm it. It wasn't any man, it was the man from the club. Looking every which way, he found no one, but he was certain. "I know you're here. I don't know where, or how, but I know you're here." He said into the darkness.

Twelve

A few steps beyond where he stood, Ari revealed himself, dropping the cloak behind him. "I'm here."

"Did you follow me?" Devlin asked, aghast and thrilled at the idea simultaneously.

"I did."

"Why?"

Ari shrugged. "I couldn't help myself. I've watched you for weeks. I couldn't let you get away. When you got up and left me, I didn't get to talk to you anymore, and I wanted to."

Devlin kicked out his hip. "I'm afraid I'm not feeling well. This really isn't the best time. Perhaps another?"

"Any that you have to give."

Devlin pulled his head back. "Really?"

Ari nodded mutely.

Devlin was awash in confusion. Of all the patrons who had come to the club, he was never the first choice, and never for conversation. For all the years surrounded by his sisters, he knew he wasn't interested in what they had to offer. But, no males he had ever encountered had interested him either. It was mighty hard to argue with himself, or anyone else, about if he was interested now, given his current state. "Why me?"

"Why not you?"

Devlin's attitude woke up. "Very true. Why not me?" It retreated as quickly and he leveled out. "But seriously, why me?"

"Perhaps you will let me list all the reasons when you have time to give me. If you are unwell, I don't want to keep you."

Devlin was nonplussed. "I can stay for a minute."

Ari beamed. "But I wish for more than a minute."

Deciding it was now or never, Devlin did something he had never done. "Look… I can't say I'm not interested, because I am. But, I'm not who you think I am."

Ari roared. "What? You are not a beautiful, graceful, limber man who dances better than every woman on the stage he shares it with?"

"You know?!" Devlin gasped.

"Did you think I could miss it?"

"But only my sisters, and Elba know."

"Then you have surrounded yourself with fools. I couldn't miss it if I tried. I knew the first time I saw you."

"Who are you?"

"I'm just a man… Just a man, looking for someone who lets me be who, and what I am. That's all."

"I'm someone."

"I certainly hope so."

Devlin sat down abruptly at the shift, not trusting himself to keep standing. "Who are you?"

"My name is Arigany."

Devlin grinned cheekily. "I'll call you Ari."

Twelve

"Everyone does. But, it sounds better when you say it." Ari replied, his voice dropping seductively as he spoke.

Devlin blushed. "You really knew the first time?"

"I was pretty sure, but didn't know until the dance tonight that you might return the interest." Ari admitted. "I was trying not to scare you off…you know, take it slow, but it was brutal. Then, I knew, but you left."

"That was awkward, huh?" Devlin blushed timidly at the memory.

"And now?" Ari asked quietly.

Devlin stared. Ari nearly folded waiting for him to answer, thinking he'd pushed too far. When Devlin found his voice, it was husky. "It's everything…wonderful, and new, and scary, and ohmygoddess…wait until my sisters find out."

Eleventh Hour

Weeks passed. Arigany was at the club every night that Devlin danced. And, every night that Devlin was in the alcove room, Ari was there to monopolize his time. Together, they learned how to keep Devlin's secret, but also Devlin learned how to resolve the situation when things 'shifted.'

Devlin's sisters and Elba had met Arigany at the household. Out of respect, he introduced himself, shared his past, and clarified his intentions. In return, they revealed their true lineage.

"I know. In the beginning, it was what brought me here." He admitted

"You came for the kingdom?" Dana challenged.

Ari held up his hands in defense. "At first, yes. I would be lying if I said otherwise. I was newly outcast and it sounded good,

Twelve

so I came, like so many others. I watched all of you for several nights before I aborted my plans."

"Which means what?" Devlin prompted, already knowing the answer, but needing his sisters to hear it.

"Which means, that it doesn't matter to me. I was a man without a home or a kingdom when I arrived, and what I gained, is worth more than what I have lost."

Aislyn smirked. Devlin caught it. "What are you thinking?"

"I'm thinking that because he doesn't want it, is all the more reason he should get it." She taunted.

"Are you thinking what I'm thinking?" Camden chimed in, a mischievous grin on her face.

"Maybe."

"It would serve him right." Camden snorted, looking from Devlin to her sisters.

"What did I do?" Devlin questioned.

"Not you him, Lyford." Aislyn clarified.

Devlin's mouth fell open. "Oh snap."

Savannah Verte

Arigany was uncomfortable with the plan, but for Devlin, he would make it work. The thirty year deadline to the amendment of the merger was set to expire at sundown. Elba led him and the twelve Rousseau children in.

Lyford was shocked to see them all. "What's wrong?" He asked, unsure what was happening, but quietly hopeful as he saw the male newcomer.

"We heard about your pledge of the Rousseau - Coeur d'Alene kingdoms to any suitor that could sway one of us to marry. We declined them all." Feraut began.

"I see." Lyford deflated.

"We've turned the tables on you, and chosen for ourselves, though only one of us is prepared to marry at this time." Dana continued.

Lyford was confused. Even knowing the plan, he defaulted with his next question. "Are they a prince?"

"Does it matter?" Raven asked pointedly.

Twelve

"I mean…" Lyford hedged, trying to figure out what was happening.

"UGH! Let's just be out with it already." Devlin cut to the chase, sauntering forward. "If he is, or if he is not doesn't matter. I am a prince."

"What?" Lyford stuttered. "You are a princess." He stated carefully.

The women all covered their eyes as Devlin dropped his trousers. "No, daddy. I. Am. A. Prince."

Lyford nearly fainted on the spot, recovering, but clinging to the back of the chair for support. Rounding on Elba, he wanted to be shouting, but could only manage to whisper. "You told me…"

"No…" Elba began. She turned to Devlin before she continued. "Pull up your trousers." Turning back to Lyford she explained. "I did not tell you. You saw the babies bundled on the bed. The blankets were discolored from all the blood, and you assumed they were pink, thus girls. Bryn tried to tell you but you shushed her. I did not tell you. What I did was choose not to relieve you of your incorrect assumption."

"But…" He stammered disbelievingly, "you could have said something at any other point."

"And you could have participated with your children at any singular moment and learned for yourself." Elba countered.

"I was overcome." He complained.

"When it was Bryn. What about when it was Ava? What about when it was Grace, my sister? If you could not find out for yourself, you cannot blame me. That fault lies at your feet."

"Grace was your sister?" He asked quietly, obviously stunned and newly saddened for the pains he had caused or failed to notice.

"Yes."

"You must hate me."

"Hate is a kind word for what I feel towards you…for her death, for how you discarded her children, for many things. I promised her I would take care of her babies, and so I have. Hers, Ava's, and even those of the only one you deigned to care for. They are the only reason I stayed."

Lyford nodded, unable to find words even close to what should be said. His shame seemed to be unending. He absently noticed the dark. The official deadline had passed, presumably as his children had intended. Looking for any flicker of redemption, he turned to them. "Not that it matters anymore, but which of you plans to marry?" Turning to Arigany, he continued. "Which of my daughters did you choose for a bride?"

Devlin moved to stand between Ari and his father. "No daddy. Once again you have it all wrong. Yes, I am a prince, but for him, I will be the Queen."

Epilogue

Devlin was revealed, and Arigany introduced, to Leopold the following day. Leopold took it all in stride. With a wink to Lyford, he officially reinstated the merger between the two kingdoms and gave his blessing to the union of the young men. They were joined, anointed, crowned, and ascended to rule over the Rousseau - Coeur d'Alene a month later. The future heir issue was left to them to figure out.

The princesses came and went from the castle more frequently, though the relationships with their father would take many years to mend. They individually returned to Logan's to dance, but the showcase of the Twelve Dancing Princesses was never seen again on the main stage. One by one they married, though none moved back into the combined kingdoms to make their homes.

Devlin and Arigany were exactly what the kingdoms needed. Ari had learned by his father's side how to rule a people with their best interests at heart, a tact that was desperately needed as they worked to rebuild the lands after the deceit and destruction of Armen that still lingered so long after his demise.

After things settled down, and a long day of work, Ari studied Devlin across the room. He wondered if his partner missed his old life. "Will you dance for me?" He tempted, trying to question if he was right.

For a moment he believed he was, frowning as Devlin replied. "Never again."

"But…"

"Never again… for anyone but you, lover. Not for anyone but you."

Twelve

Acknowledgements

There never seem to be enough pages to properly thank everyone who makes this crazy journey possible. I could not do this without any of them.

First, to my PA Jennifer who stares me down in the face of the manic and says again and again, 'You've got this.'

Second, to the person who takes my zoo-ish first drafts, and sends back something that resembles what I wanted to put out to begin with, but didn't quite accomplish, for my editor Shelly…you cannot possibly know your value to my writing world.

Most importantly, to my family…the blood ones, the author tribe who support me, and the readers who continue to delve into the alphabet soup on paper that is my story-psycho come to life…there will *NEVER* be enough Thank You to go around. You make this adventure worth the sleepless nights and road time. I cannot possibly ever do you justice, or thank you for all that you give me.

If you enjoyed Savannah's brand of storytelling, consider checking out her other tales:

The Custos Series
Book of Time
Book of Change
Book of Mysteries
Book of Revelations

Flip-Flopped Fairy Tales
Imposs-i-Bella
Twelve

Tales in 13 Chapters
Immortal Deflagration
Immortal Alchemy
Veil Break

Una-mor Trilogy
Rogue
Black Guard
Assissins

Paranormal Dating Agency
Baiting A Berserker
Grow Some Gills
Kiss My Splash

H.E.A.R.T. Flights
Liftoff

Stand alone titles:
C.A.S.E. Revelations
Gravedigger
Viva Zapata & the Magic 8-Ball
Georgia Roots Revealed
(with Debut Author Shelly Small)

LINKS CAN BE FOUND AT
www.savannahverte.com/books

About the Author

A lifelong lover of words and reading, Savanah Verte hasn't quite figured out what she wants to write when she grows up. Born and raised in the upper Midwest, Savannah's gypsy spirit and never quit attitude keep her busy and seldom idle. For so many reasons, Savannah considers herself a 'Contemporary Vagabond' when it comes to writing and hopes that others find her diverse offerings as enjoyable to read as they are to write.

As the primary owner and driving force behind Eclectic Bard Books, she considers herself immensely fortunate to see writing from varied perspectives as she endeavors to publish the authors rostered there. Working with other writers, Savannah gets to expand her horizons every day as someone brings a new idea to the table and the brainstorming begins. There is something addictive about the creative process for her and helping other authors embrace their dreams make hers a reality daily.

Follow Savannah:
www.savannahverte.com
www.facebook.com/authorsavannahverte
www.eclecticbardbooks.com/savannahverte

Peek at Another Flip-Flopped Fairy Tale

Imposs-i-Bella

Bippity…Boppity…Balance.

We all know how Cinderella went to the ball, met her prince, lost a shoe, and got her happily ever after…but did you know that for such a magical thing to occur the universe demands a price? As a matter of fact, an equal measure in return.

Isabella Beaufort was born at the top of the social food chain. She had everything, including being promised to Prince Christopher, until the ill-fated ball where he met Cinderella. Follow along as we learn about the other side of the rags to riches story we all know, and the price of pissing off a fairy godmother.

Imposs-I-Bella
Chapter 1

Flora took in the scene from her alcove near the window, staying to the periphery. The baby to be born would be her charge. Judging by the state of the grand affair, this child would not need her. People were tripping over themselves to offer goods and services to the family, though the family wasn't in the room. By her count, it was about time she got an easy case anyway. Being a Fairy Godmother was hard work.

The child wailed a blistering scream just after the resounding smack across its bottom was heard. Wincing, she had to give it credit, the child had lungs. Flora withdrew her fingers from her ears after several moments and waited for the pronouncement.

"It's a girl." Was announced loudly to the waiting crowd in the ante-chamber beyond the birthing quarter's door, by a less than enthusiastic servant whose head disappeared just as abruptly as it had appeared. The crowd erupted.

It was not a secret. The house desperately needed a female young if there was to be any hope of salvaging the family name. Generations of males had all but run the reputation into the ground. A stockpile had been secreted away ages ago for just this moment. Before long, there would be pledges and promises, and a handsome dowry to a male of worth. Flora wondered off-hand whom would be chosen, and just how long it might take. She guessed the marriage bargain would be made before the child could walk.

Hours later, the young's moniker was announced as the child was presented; Isabella Reede Esme Catherine Renee Beaufort. Flora decided immediately that she would call her Bella. That was that.

Approaching the parents once they appeared, Flora bowed and gave her blessings, introduced herself, and left for the nursery to await the child. There was no need to linger, she knew exactly what was coming. A great vat of wine had already been opened and was being poured long before the family emerged from the birthing chambers. There would be drinking and merriment, singing and speculating, posturing and promises…then there would be a screaming child delivered to the nursery. Flora was going to get her break before she couldn't.

As expected, the girl arrived shortly, wailing for all she was worth in the arms of the nursemaid. Flora inspected her carefully, knowing immediately that her earlier assessment was wrong, this child would be a handful, her obsidian eyes twinkled with mischief already. It did not escape Flora's notice that this child was her own nemesis as she had cleaved a tuft of her own hair and was pulling.

"No wonder you're wailing. I'd cry too if someone were tugging at my hair." She chided the squalling baby.

"I hardly think…" the nursemaid began, cutting herself short when she noticed whom she addressed. "I beg your pardon. Would you care to hold her?"

"No, no. I'll leave that to you." Flora retorted with a smug grin as she pointed to her own chest. "Perk of position. You swaddle and soothe, I get to try to keep her out of trouble for the next eighteen years. I daresay, judging by right now, I'll have my hands plenty full of her before too long. Isn't that right Miss Bella?" She finished her comments to the child directly who almost seemed to narrow her eyes in reply.

The nursemaid didn't seem affronted until Flora called the girl 'Bella,' at which she tried to spin away. "You should at least learn her name." she admonished.

"I know her name." Flora responded softly, even as her hand shot out to halt the spin with force. "But I, unlike you, am not her servant."

Twelve

The nursemaid's sharp intake of breath was not quiet. "If....if...if you won't help me with her, then perhaps you will give her some peace. Being born into this world has surely exhausted her. You can leave." She said on a raspy, harsh whisper.

Flora laughed loudly. For a moment, Bella quieted at the sound. It was short-lived. Though the child resumed her screaming, Flora's face was calm, nearly stoic, before she spoke. "Hear me clearly; I will leave when I wish, and stay when I wish. And, though you may not always see me, I am watching. I do not answer to you any more than I answer to the child in your arms. Do you understand?"

The maid nodded mutely, her jaw slack at the rebuke.

"I'm glad we cleared that up. And thank you, I do believe I'll go now. This evening has been taxing." Flora announced before turning to leave.

Turning back, she smirked at the maid with an odd giggle. "Silly me...as if I need to leave through the door." She announced before spiraling her finger into the air and disappearing, waiting until she was out of sight to laugh at the expression on the maid's face as she went. She only narrowly managed it. The sound bubbled up to her lips with such force she nearly didn't hold the outburst.

Fern was seated in her favorite chair, flipping the pages of a book she wasn't reading when Flora returned. Her sister was nearly cackling at something, though it was in conflict with the steam that seemed to rise off of her in thick tufts.

"Whatever is going on?" Fern queried as she looked up.

"Just enjoying the reaction." Flora retorted off-hand, waving off further questions.

Fern studied her, not taking the hint. "You got your new assignment then did you?"

"You know I did." Flora quipped, almost snapping the words out. "You're next you know." She wagged a finger.

"Yes, I know." Fern said calmly, turning yet another page she wasn't looking at. "I believe it will be tomorrow though. Maybe."

"What makes you say that?" Flora glared.

Fern heaved a hard sigh and closed the book. "It's not going well. Breech."

Flora gasped at the one word that said it all. "We can share mine." She offered lamely.

Fern shrugged it off. "We'll see."

Made in the USA
Lexington, KY
18 August 2018